The QUEEN of COOL

Cecil Castellucci

CANDLEWICK PRESS
CAMBRIDGE, MASSACHUSETTS

Shout-outs to Mom and Dad; the menagerie I call or have called my friends; the Los Angeles Zoo—Luz Morales and Mike Dee; The Little People of America (LPA) Los Angeles Chapter; Kerry Slattery, Steve Salardino, and Skylight Books; my landlords, Bernard and Diana Arias; my gentle readers, Jo Knowles, Patty Cornell, Rob Takata, Sarah Sprague; Andrea Kleine, Katrina Kemp, and Keith Martin; my LA Lit Ladies, Jen Sincero and Carolyn Kellogg; the Cult of B and my other fellow author friends; my agent, Barry "Mr. Fantastic" Goldblatt; my Candlewick peeps; and most of all, my editor, friend, and the true Queen of Cool, the divine Ms. Kara LaReau

Copyright © 2006 by Cecil Castellucci

First paperback edition 2007

The Library of Congress has cataloged the hardcover edition as follows:
Castellucci, Cecil, date.
The queen of cool / Cecil Castellucci. — 1st ed.
p.   cm.
Summary: Bored with her life, popular high school junior Libby signs up for an internship at the zoo and discovers that the "science nerds" she meets there may have a few things to teach her about friendship and life.
ISBN 978-0-7636-2720-1 (hardcover)
[1. Self-perception—Fiction. 2. Conduct of life—Fiction. 3. Zoos—Fiction. 4. High schools—Fiction. 5. Schools—Fiction.]   I. Title.
PZ7.C26865Que 2006
[Fic]—dc22   2005050174

ISBN 978-0-7636-3413-1 (paperback)

2 4 6 8 10 9 7 5 3 1

Printed in the United States of America

This book was typeset in Plantin.

Candlewick Press
2067 Massachusetts Avenue
Cambridge, Massachusetts 02140

visit us at www.candlewick.com

To all you rare birds

1.

Weekday morning routine:
Take shower.
Assemble perfect outfit.
Apply makeup.
Pull hair into bun. Secure with glitter
pencils.
Accept twenty-dollar bill from Dad.
Pick up latte and creamy chocolate
brioche from café.
Drive to school the long way.
Listen to sad music way too loud.
Nab choice parking spot under tree.

When I enter the school courtyard, Perla waves me over with her mascara wand, then continues to apply her makeup. She needs no mirror. She knows her own face by heart.

"Morning, Libby," she says, concentrating on her eyelashes, not looking at me. "Cute outfit."

"It should be cute," I say. "I worked hard to come up with it."

I may not be as devastatingly gorgeous as Perla, but I know how to emphasize my assets.

I plop my bag on the ground and sit in the middle of my friends:

Kenji, frantically copying some homework before the bell rings.

Perla, now blotting her lips on the corner of the weekly school handout.

Sid, his nose in a book, his ears plugged up with headphones, his head bouncing slightly in and out of his green hooded sweatshirt.

Mike Dutko, head leaning against the trunk of the tree, half asleep, mouth open.

"Brainstorm," I say.

Everyone stops what they are doing to look at me.

"You must create your own fun," I say as I pull the glitter pencils out of my hair and tape them onto my shirt.

Sid removes his headphones and pulls his hood back to make the announcement.

"Pencil Day!"

Perla laughs. Kenji digs into his bag and starts looking for pencils.

Halfway through the day, everyone has covered themselves with pens or pencils.

Halfway through the day, the tape no longer has the strength to keep the pencils in their place, and they start to drop off my shirt. They are jumping ship. The pencils are bailing.

They might just have the right idea.

I think: Fuck it.

Out of school. Out of mind.

I cut and go home.

2.

"Ugh, that little freak freaks me out," Perla says during Nutrition.

I look over to where she's pointing. It's at Tiny Carpentieri. She's over by the vending machine getting an apple.

I don't like the look of Tiny either. She's too, I dunno, *desperate*.

When the bell rings, she passes by us. She kicks her right leg out a little bit when she walks.

"She waddles like a duck," Perla says.

"She's not a *duck*. She's a *dwarf*."

I'm not even being funny. Or mean. I'm just being truthful. Tiny is a dwarf.

"Weird Walk Day," Perla announces, and walks to class shaking her ass the whole way.

I take quick little steps, which make me fall behind. Perla laughs and tells me to hurry up.

By the end of the day, everyone in school is doing a weird walk.

By the end of the day, the teachers are asking everyone to stop it.

By the end of the day, I am over it. It was so second period.

3.

"What do you think the point of life is?" I ask.

We are sitting in my rec room. I'm swigging a beer. Mike Dutko is passing around a joint.

No one says a word, until Sid pipes up.

"Life is everything and nothing. Wonderful and terrible. The beginning and the end."

Perla laughs.

"You are such a *dork*," Perla says. It's her favorite insult this week. Last week it was *moron*.

"Yeah, man, school just started, and already you're reading way too many books," Mike Dutko says.

Of course, they're trying to get a rise out of Sid. Everyone does. Sid is such an easy target.

But Sid does not engage. He folds his hands in front of him and presses his full lips into a thin line.

"Life is a pain in my ass," Perla says, raising up her beer in a toast. "Give me oblivion!"

Mike Dutko laughs and pulls Perla close to him. In a minute he will go to the bathroom and ask Perla to help him with something.

And then she will give him a hand job.

I will be stuck sitting in my rec room alone with Sid, and he and I will attempt small talk. Out of embarrassment, we will not look at each other because we will know what is really going on in the bathroom.

Sid will talk to me about his band, Swisher.

Or he will talk about some obscure book he is reading.

Or he will mention a philosophical thing that no one has ever heard about.

He will try to fill up the air with words so that we can't hear the noises coming from the bathroom.

It's the same old routine.

Mike Dutko makes his move, but before Perla follows him, Kenji finally arrives, followed by a bunch of other kids from school. He is carrying a case of beer.

"I've brought reinforcements!" Kenji says. "Let's get this party started!"

Kenji wedges himself between Sid and me. He puts his arm around my waist.

Sid looks relieved by the sudden invasion.

I know I am.

4.

Of course, Pajama Day is my idea.

I am wearing Gama-Go pajamas and toting around Mr. Puffy, my teddy bear from when I was a kid.

Perla is wearing a fancy lace nightgown.

Sid is wearing crisply ironed, blue-striped vintage pajamas.

Mike Dutko forgot about the whole plan.

Kenji is wearing a robe.

"I sleep naked," he explains.

A week later, Perla snorts and points at a bunch of total geeks who show up to school wearing pajamas. I notice Tiny Carpentieri is wearing a Disneyland Sleeping Beauty T-shirt, only on her it reaches all the way to the floor.

"Copycats," Perla says, snapping her gum and adjusting her bra under her flamingo pink baby-tee that has the words *Spoiled Brat* printed in rhinestones across her boobs.

Her every move results in a disco effect, creating a

bunch of mini-rainbows on the wall of lockers next to us. I'm mesmerized, but Perla's already moved on to the next topic: boys and how they all love her.

"God, they all stare at me," she says. "I guess it's good practice for when I'm famous, when my dad gives me my own reality show, *The Totally True Adventures of a Beautiful Girl.*"

"Is that what it's going to be called?" I ask.

"I don't know—I'm trying it out," she says.

It is true; she is beautiful.

Everybody stares at Perla. Even babies. Even old women. Everybody. And I know what they think—I can see it in their faces: "My God, what a lovely girl."

I zone out again and watch the rhinestone rainbows shimmer in time with her body while she counts on both hands, twice, all the boys she swears get a boner whenever she walks by.

". . . and Mr. Stephens. He's always, like, adjusting himself around me."

Perla finishes her list and stops moving. The rainbows disappear, along with my moment of inner peace.

I snap shut the lock on my locker.

From somewhere behind me, I overhear someone say what a cool idea coming to school in your pajamas is.

Usually I would turn around and demand credit where credit is due. But who has the energy to care?

5.

The late bell rings, and I just make it into AP Biology on time.

"Find a seat, please, Libby," Ms. Lew says.

I scan the room and notice two empty seats. One is next to Kenji and Sid in the back of the room. Kenji is making kissy faces at me. The other seat is in the front row with the total rejects.

I make my way over to the boys and sit down. I am not in the mood for my boys today. But I just can't do dork.

Ms. Lew, an aspiring actress who can hardly fake being interested in teaching us, places her hands on the back of her chair and sighs heavily.

I bet we are the closest thing she ever comes to having an audience.

She turns and writes the words *Endangered Species* on the board in dry erase marker. She's picked the color red. I can tell this is going to be a dramatic class.

"The world is in ecological crisis. Who can guess some of the causes for endangerment?" she asks.

A handful of kids in the front of the room raise their hands.

"Tina," Ms. Lew says as she calls on Tiny.

"Causes could include habitat, or the introduction of a new exotic species into the environment."

Showoff.

I wonder if Tiny *has* to sit in the front of the room because she can't see over anybody's head if she sits anywhere else. I wonder if that's why she always raises her hand. I wonder if the classroom looks different from the front of the room. I bet it's harder to not pay attention.

"Good, Tina," Ms. Lew says. "Anyone else? Libby? You have a look of deep thought on your face. Do you have anything to add?"

"Me?" I ask. I hate being singled out in class.

"No thoughts at all?"

"None I care to share," I say.

People laugh. Ms. Lew is not happy.

"How about overexploitation?" Sid calls out.

I turn to look at him as he acts the hero, thinking he's saved my ass. He hasn't. I could've come up with an acceptable answer. If I really wanted to.

"Good. How about some examples?" Ms. Lew says.

"Well, like people who think tiger bones will make them virile," Sid says.

People laugh. Louder.

I notice that Sid is not laughing. The word *virile* doesn't make him crack a smile.

9

"Excellent," Ms. Lew says, her mood brightening a bit. She probably feels good about her performance today.

She starts writing down a million notes on the board. Pulling down maps. Handing out info sheets. She is excited.

But me, I am ready for a nap.

I open my loose-leaf notebook, propping it up in front of me. Then I put my head down on the desk.

It smells like pencil and hand.

6.

SWISHER is scrawled in Sharpie pen across the chest of my homemade T-shirt, which I've cut up strategically to show just enough flesh.

Swisher, like the toilet and faucet maker, is the name of Sid's band, which is on stage in the middle of their third song.

Swisher is what makes Sid cool enough to pal around with us.

Swisher has no singer. The music is like a physical attack. It moves from a delicate whisper of notes to a full-throttled cacophony. I join the throng of people dancing in the pit.

I want to lose myself in the music. I want to feel free.

I want to feel *something*.

I try to dance myself into a frenzy until sweat is pouring down my sides and my makeup feels like it's running off my face. I close my eyes. I feel the same. Empty. Maybe I just need a beer.

I go to the bathroom and splash myself with water. I take out my travel-size rubbing alcohol and I wipe off the under-21 stamps the bouncer put on the backs of my hands.

I sidle up to the bar.

"A draft beer, please," I say.

The bartender pulls on the tap and slides the beer over to me without a second thought. He doesn't bother asking me for my ID. He just looks at the backs of my unmarked hands.

I walk back over to Perla. She's sweaty from the dancing.

"*Chica!* Where'd you get that beer?" she asks.

"The bar," I say. "Suckers."

"Give me a sip," Perla says.

I hand her the cup. She drinks it stealthily, but she holds the cup as though it belongs in her hands. She's had practice.

After the show, Sid and his band load the gear out of the club while the rest of us go straight over to Jakob's and steal some pinot grigio and shiraz from his dad's wine cellar.

"This is a good year," Mike Dutko says, nodding in approval at the label, trying to sound like he knows something.

"Just fucking uncork it," I say.

Sid and his bandmates show up two bottles later. I am already warm and drunk from all the wine and the music. I am sitting between Mike Dutko and Sid. Perla is across the room making out with Jakob.

Kenji and I have an understanding. And Kenji is not out with us tonight. So I have a choice.

I could choose to make out with Mike Dutko, 'cause he's available for the smooching. Or I could choose to make out with Sid.

However, I am not drunk enough to make out with Sid. I will never be drunk enough for that. Even though his band doesn't suck, Perla and I agree that he has absolutely no sex appeal.

"Let's play spin-the-bottle," Perla says, like she always does, 'cause she thinks that sometimes a girl just needs to get drunk and make out with cute boys.

Always game for a chance to exchange fluids with Perla, Mike Dutko drains one of the bottles and places it on the floor.

"You playing?" he asks me with bedroom eyes.

"No," I say.

I move myself out of the ring and pour myself another drink.

"Suit yourself," he says, and twists the bottle with a flick of his wrist.

But before the spinning bottle on the floor has a chance to stop, I see Sid uncross his legs and remove himself from the circle too. He heads away from me, toward the CD player, closer to the speakers. For Sid, there is always safety in music.

From the other side of the room I watch everyone else in the ring. They chuckle and chortle and whoop as the bottle doles out the random kisses.

I play my own game. Desert Island.

7.

"What time did you get home last night?" Mom says. "Sounded late."

"Five a.m."

"Did you have fun?" Dad asks.

"Yep," I say.

"Pass me the sports section," Dad says.

I hand it over and pour myself another cup of coffee.

"So how's your weekend looking?" Mom asks Dad.

"Work," Dad grunts.

"Can you expand on that?" Mom asks.

"Gotta come up with copy for a new low-carb, fat-free chocolate bar," he says.

"Does it taste good?" I ask.

"No, of course it doesn't taste *good*," Dad says, rolling his eyes. "It tastes like cardboard."

"We have tickets to the opera," Mom reminds him.

"I'm working. Take Libby," he says.

"I'm busy," I say.

"Well," Mom says to no one in particular, "it seems like a waste."

Dad peers over the paper at Mom. "Take one of your friends from work."

"I wanted to go with *you*," she says. "Never mind. I'll donate them back to theater. Someone can use them, I'm sure."

"Give them to Nastja," Dad suggests.

"I'm not sure Nastja would like the opera," Mom says.

"Why wouldn't she?" I ask.

"Because she's the cleaning lady," Dad says.

"I didn't say that," Mom says. "Mitch, don't put words in my mouth."

"Have you asked her?"

"No, but maybe I will," she says. "Why do you have to be like this?"

"Like what?" he asks.

"So . . . irritable."

I push myself away from the table. I don't *have* to excuse myself, but just to be *polite,* I announce that I'm going to my room.

The parental units take no notice of me as I make my leave. They are too busy having a *discussion.*

I scan my bedroom for a mid-morning activity.

Red Fender Telecaster guitar in corner of room.

Panasonic DV camera.

Easel, paints, canvas, papers, good light through window.

Library books.

I like the idea of them all. But not one of these things really captures my imagination. I just can't see myself actually doing any of them.

I don't want to make the effort. Just give me the end result, I say.

Thinking of the energy any one of those things would require makes me immediately want to lie down.

I throw myself on my bed and take a nap.

8.

Ass Backward Day.

Sid is adjusting his pants. They are bothering him because he's put his vintage lime green 1970s polyester suit on backward *and* inside out.

Kenji yanks at the lapels.

"Why do you always have to do this?" Kenji asks Sid.

"What?"

"Overdo it."

Kenji is only wearing his T-shirt backward, but it doesn't even look like it's backward. It looks like it's supposed to be worn that way. It's obvious Kenji is just jealous of Sid for being more creative than him.

"One should always try to 'overdo it,'" Sid says.

"Who said that? Confucius?" Kenji laughs.

"No, Confucius said—"

"Sid, tell me, do you have to use your big brain to hide your micropenis?" Kenji laughs again.

"Nice, Kenji," I say.

"I've got an idea," Perla says, refocusing the attention back to her, as always.

"Your ideas always suck," Kenji says.

16

"What about Weird Walk Day?" Perla says. "That was my idea. That was a great idea, right Libby?"

"You just copied Tiny. That's unoriginal," I reply.

"Whatever," Perla says, putting her hand in front of her like a stop sign. "Can I help it if Tiny walked by at that moment and *inspired* me?"

Perla will never admit that *I'm* the idea girl. *I'm* the original thinker. *She's* the copycat. But I just don't see the point of getting my panties all in a stitch today, so I don't bother reminding her.

"Her name is Tina," Sid says. His panties *are* in a stitch.

But no one acts like they hear him.

"Okay, I got one," Perla says. "How about No Makeup-Wearing Day?"

"Yeah, that's dumb, Perla," Kenji says. "Guys don't wear makeup, and most girls don't wear as much makeup as you. Like, *not at all.*"

"Well, at least it was an *idea*," Perla says, pulling out her compact and applying lip-gloss. Her enormous lips always look moist and glittery. "I don't hear anyone else speaking."

"We have bigger things to think about than what we're going to do for fun tomorrow," I say.

"Like what?" Perla asks.

"Like the Fall Formal," I say. "I think we should be color coordinated."

"Right!" Perla says.

"And there should be no dates," Kenji says. "We go as a group."

"Like an orgy," Mike says.

"We'll all wear purple," I say.

"But the theme is Autumn Fires," Perla says. "We'll clash with the decorations."

"That's the point," I say.

"Oh," she says. "I get it."

But clearly, she doesn't.

9.

We're all outside, behind the gym. I'm in a fabulous purple gown sucking vodka and grape punch through a straw. Perla is smoking a cigarette, trying to look glamorous in long lavender gloves.

"This shit is awkward," she says. She peels off the gloves, finger by finger.

Why is it that when you have what seems to be the perfect combination of elements to ensure no-brainer fun—friends, booze, music, and fancy clothes—you still all end up in a yawn fest, standing around behind the gym, complaining?

The vodka isn't working. It's not strong enough. Suddenly I know what will give me the buzz I need.

I start peeling off my dress.

"What are you doing?" Perla says. "*Chica,* put your dress back on."

The boys don't say anything. They continue to drink the punch and try to look like they are not looking at me, the girl standing in front of them in her bra and underwear.

"I dare you to go inside like that," Kenji says.

"That's the plan," I say.

He puts his hands around my waist and pulls me toward him.

"That's my girl," he says, kissing me.

When I break away from him, there is a string of saliva still connecting me to his mouth. It glistens in the light, then breaks and falls onto his chin.

I wipe it off with my thumb.

"Anyone care to join me?" I ask.

Not one of them meets my eyes. They all shake their heads no.

Wimps. All of them.

"What will you do when you get to the other side?" Perla says. "You'll be, like, naked."

I grab a plastic bag from the garbage and put my dress and shoes in it.

"Ready," I say.

"Wait," Sid says. He goes back to the garbage can and digs through until he finds a paper bag. He rips two eyeholes in it and places it over my head. "You don't want to get caught."

They open the door and go into the gym while I hang back.

I count to ten. My heart is pounding.

"GO!" I tell myself.

I push the door open and start to run. I see almost nothing. A flash of fabric. An ogling face. The sound of shrieks. A cackle. An adult screaming to stop me.

But I am still running, past the jocks and the cheerleaders and the math club and the vogue girls and the sun and surfers and the extremers and the young politicos. It is me and my feet on the floor and my goal: the doors at the other side of the gym.

I make it.

I run down the hallway right into the bathroom and dive into a stall. I take the brown bag off my head and let my hair spill out as I lean my head forward. I put my face in my sweaty hands.

Instead of laughing or feeling thrilled, I have to bite the inside of my cheeks to keep from crying.

What is wrong with me?

I feel no difference from that moment of running to this moment of crying, and the next one, the one where I open my garbage bag and calmly put my dress back on.

Shit. I'm missing a shoe.

10.

I wake up on Monday morning, and my bedroom is the same, and the view outside the window is the same, and the smell of breakfast coming up from down the hall is the same. Only *I* feel different.

At lunchtime, in the pavilion, I sit at the usual table, and I am eating the same lunch I have every day (fat-free, sugar-free yogurt and a Diet Coke), while everyone else is talking over one another.

They are all *talking*. And nobody is *listening*.

Kenji: "I refuse to go to museums because they're just trying to dictate what culture *is*, but once it's in a museum, all they're doing is displaying what culture *was*. And by that time it's dead."

Perla: "Why would I bother with acting school? Such a waste of time. Everybody knows that reality shows are the way to become a megastar."

Sid: "The best band to ever come out of Seattle is

Mudhoney, not Nirvana. It's such a cop-out to say Nirvana."

Mike Dutko: "That chick's boobs look good in that sweater."

All of a sudden it hits me.

I don't want to say it out loud because I really can't believe it, but it's true.

They're all *boring*.

Everything is boring.

"What's wrong with you, Libby?" Perla asks. "You sick?"

"No," I say.

"You look sick. Like pale white or something."

"Bad yogurt," I say. I get up and throw the container into the garbage can.

I'm not hungry.

I'm not anything.

Thankfully, the bell rings and it's time to go to AP Biology.

I rush to class. I practically run. Not because I'm going to be late, and not because I even care about getting there on time, but just because I want to get away from my friends.

I'm afraid that they'll all find out what's really wrong with me.

Outside the classroom, I'm panting with my head down and my hands on my knees. I wonder if I'm having a heart attack. I look up and try to focus on something, on the internship bulletin board with its even blocks of pastel-colored flyers. I read the big black cutout letters on top of the board that say *Are You Ready for an Adventure in SCIENCE?*

The word *SCIENCE* is wobbling. It looks as though it's 3-D. It's jumping out at me.

I stand in front of the bulletin board for a long time. People jostle me as they pass by to go into the classroom. I steady myself by keeping my eyes on the internship sign-up sheet for the L.A. Zoo.

That's something I would *never* do.

Scientifically speaking, I'm not a scientist.

But before I know what I am doing, my pen is out of my bag and with my shaking hand I am signing the sheet.

I sign at the top, on the first line. Number one. I almost think that I'm going to be the only one who signs up when I notice that the bottom line is filled out too.

Number 25. Tina Carpentieri.

I laugh. She probably couldn't reach any higher.

11.

It takes only one day for Ms. Lew to call my name at the end of biology class.

"Libby, can I talk to you a moment?" Ms. Lew asks.

I know why she wants to talk to me. I want to leave so that I can cross my name off the list hanging outside of her classroom door.

"Yeah, I really have to get to class. I don't want to be late."

Usually this tactic works. But today Ms. Lew writes out a late pass for me. I put my book bag down on a desk.

"I just wanted to let you know how pleased I am that you've signed up for the L.A. Zoo internship," she says.

"I'm going to quit."

"But it hasn't even started," she says.

"Yeah, I might have been temporarily insane," I say.

She smiles. She thinks I'm kidding. Making a joke. She doesn't know I'm actually worried that it might be true. I may be insane. My name on that paper may have been the only thing keeping me from becoming a quivering blob outside her classroom yesterday.

"I wish you wouldn't quit. You excel in science."

"No, I don't excel in anything. I'm a B student."

"I think we both know that you can get a B with your eyes closed."

"No, I struggle," I say. But no matter how serious I try to look, I can't help smiling.

"It counts as an extra science class," she adds. "And it will look terrific on your college applications next year."

I want to say, *BIG WHOOP.* But Ms. Lew is being sincere and passionate again, and I just don't have the heart to be shitty to her.

"Okay," I say.

"Libby, this is a good opportunity. It shows initiative. You are a natural leader, and thanks to you, other students have signed up for some science internships too."

"I didn't mean to start a trend," I say.

"Well, you did."

The late bell rings.

"I gotta go, Ms. Lew."

"I'm giving you a compliment, Libby. Try to learn to accept compliments."

She turns back to her desk, and I figure I can finally leave. I get to the door, and I turn back and I say one more thing.

"Thank you, Ms. Lew."

But I don't know why I said it. I know I'm not thankful for a single thing.

12.

I cut American History class and go to the bleachers by the track so I can try to finish *The Great Gatsby*. Maybe if I get my reading done, I will actually bother showing up for English.

The field is full of football players running into mats, soccer players bouncing balls on knees, and track people running around the field. Except one girl. She's in the middle of the field doing yoga. Downward facing dog. Sun salutation. Tree pose. It looks awkward, though. Her body is all wrong. After a minute, I realize it's not the shapes that she twists in that make her body look all wrong. It's Tiny. And Tiny's body is strange. Her hips are a bit too wide. Her legs are just a bit too short. Her arms bend over her trunk a bit too soon.

She's completely oblivious to all of the grunting and shouting and running around her. She sits down and starts to meditate.

I shade my eyes to watch her. She's more interesting than the book I'm not reading. She's almost graceful in a way. Once you get used to watching her movements, they somehow make sense.

Perla, who cuts class as much as I do, approaches.

Her long, shiny, black hair is pulled back into a Frida Kahlo braid that swings from side to side as she joins me on the bleachers.

She stands in front of me, blocking my view of Tiny and her interesting stretching, so I put my head down and begin reading again.

"I have to cheat," Perla says. "Reading all those words makes my brain hurt."

"Mmm-hmm," I say. "Sounds like the smart thing to do."

Of course she totally misses the sarcasm in my voice.

"I know, right? Sid sits next to me, so I just cheat off him. Except I have to reword his weird concepts so it sounds like I wrote it. But at least then I know I'll get an automatic C."

"Doesn't it ever bore you not to think, Perla?" I ask.

Ironically, she has to think about it.

13.

"Aw, man!" Kenji says. "Why'd you sign up for a winter session internship?"

"Because," I say.

"Not coo'," Kenji says. "No fun. Total snore pie."

He tilts his head sideways as though he's falling asleep and makes snoring sounds.

"I think it's stupid," Mike Dutko says.

"A total waste of time," Perla says.

"Basically, it blows," Kenji says, one hand on my thigh, and the other hand making its way down my shirt. "I don't understand why you're doing it. It's for geeks."

I don't say anything. I twist away from Kenji.

"Where you going?" he says.

I reach into the Halloween candy bowl on the glass coffee table. It's an excuse to get away from his slithering hands.

Strange. The more that they say it's the *wrong* thing to do, the more I *want* to do it.

"It's only for winter session," I say. "Three months. Starts in December, ends by spring break."

I look at them:

Kenji, stretching out his legs, kicking his snakeskin boots up on the coffee table.

Perla, in her pink feather sweater, staring blankly as she applies her lipstick for the fourth time in half an hour.

Mike Dutko, preoccupied with the Band-Aid on his hairy finger.

Sid, wearing vintage tortoiseshell glasses, peering out from underneath his sweatshirt hood. He thinks I don't notice that he's the only one looking at me and that he's the only one who hasn't weighed in either way.

He's waiting for the explanation.

Then it dawns on me.

"There are these crabs in the ocean," I begin. "They get into a fisherman's net, and they're too stupid to get out. They just can't figure it out. But every once in a while, one crab figures out how to escape, and the other crabs go crazy and pull it back into the net; they pull its arms and legs off because they just don't want it to leave."

"I guess you're *not* napping in science class," Sid says.

"Are you calling me a crab?" Kenji asks.

I don't say anything.

"Whatever," Perla says, momentarily done with her preening. "She'll still have plenty of time to hang out. How hard can it be? It's the zoo. It's just animals."

"Exactly," I say, looking at all of them. "Animals."

14.

Perla comes up to me between sixth and seventh period as I'm getting my textbook out of my locker.

"I have to baby-sit my cousin after school," she says. "I pulled the family short straw."

She puts her fingers in the form of an *L* on her forehead. The sign of the Loser.

"Well, I have a thing to do too. I have orientation at the zoo," I say.

"Oh that. Can't you skip it? I don't want to baby-sit alone."

"Uhm. I can't."

Perla pouts and bats her eyes.

"Not going to work on me," I say. "Try it on Mike Dutko."

"Ooh. That's a good idea. He'd do anything for me. He *loves* me."

She grins, making her finger pop out and up. The sign of the Boner.

The chair is hard as a rock, and the plastic digs into my back. Though I am uncomfortable, I try to seem engaged. When will Mrs. Torres, the animal services manager, get to the part where I can pay attention? All I can focus on is the tacky alligator earrings she is wearing.

At last she starts saying something interesting.

"Strict hygiene rules are in place here at the zoo due to diseases like mad cow and Newcastle virus."

I shudder. The horror. She blah blah blahs more about the animals and the importance of hygiene.

"The condor is an endangered species. It is a California native, and it is a bird of prey," Mrs. Torres says. "The public never sees the birds. We only breed them."

I look around wondering if anyone is as startled as I

am. What a sad life those endangered birds must have. Kept away from public eyes. Never free. A life secluded for the one chance of species survival. I shudder again.

"Cold?" Tiny asks. "Me too. I'm always cold. I'll go ask them to turn down the air conditioning."

Tiny climbs off her chair and talks to an animal service technician in the back of the room, who makes an adjustment on the thermostat.

I can't believe it. I bet she totally played the dwarf card with that guy.

On her way back, she squeezes the arm of a geeky kid with a pizza face. He turns bright red and smiles at her. Then Tiny makes her way back over to her chair.

I wish she hadn't sat next to me. Just because we go to the same school doesn't make us automatic friends. She's totally going to try to be buddy-buddy with me. I can tell.

"We do not ever work with any animals directly. They are off limits," warns Mrs. Torres.

I raise my hand.

"Excuse me," I say.

"Yes, Miss . . ."

"Brin," I say. "Libby Brin."

"Libby. Go ahead."

"I don't understand. We don't *ever* get to touch the animals?"

"If you had read your paperwork, you would have

seen that unless interns are eighteen years old, they are not allowed near any animals. You can clean cages. You can help with animal enrichment. You can and will learn biology. But these are WILD ANIMALS."

"Well, what's the point . . . ?"

"No one has *you* in a cage, Libby. You can leave the zoo at any time. There's the exit."

The other interns, not one of which looks at all cool, begin to laugh.

They are laughing at *me*!

Mrs. Torres waits to see what I will do before she starts talking again.

I cross my arms and make a big show of getting comfortable in my chair. When it's clear I'm not leaving, she nods and continues.

"The procedure will be as follows: A team member will check in and receive your daily assignment. You will do whatever the animal keeper asks you to do. Your team will be required to take notes of your activities. You will be graded on these field books. You will be on duty with a different animal every week. When you are done with the internship, should you choose to continue with us here at the zoo, you will have had training enough to move on to the next level and apprentice with a specific kind of exotic animal."

"Sometimes I don't know how I feel about zoos," Tiny says, twisting toward me. "But at least it's better here than that old zoo. Have you ever been there? I mean, to the old zoo? Seen those tiny empty cages?"

"No," I manage to respond.

"It's just on the other side of the park. We should go one day. It's really thought-provoking."

Whatever.

Thankfully Mrs. Torres interrupts before I have to figure out some kind of an excuse. Normally I don't feel as though I need to come up with one; I can just say *NO.* But Tiny is relentless. She seems like the kind of person who needs reasons.

"Now I will hand out your team assignments," Mrs. Torres announces. "These will be your teams for the duration of the internship. Green Team will be Matthew Avilles, Consuela Adams, and Priscilla Brand. Blue Team will be Libby Brin, Sheldon Black, and Tina Carpentieri . . ."

Tiny smiles at me. Then she turns around and gives the thumbs-up to Pizza Face in the back of the room. That must be Sheldon Black.

Great. I'm on Team Loser. Not that there is anybody else's team that seems to be any better. If I ever had any worries about my being uncool, they evaporate with one quick scan of the room. It's like, which shade of awful would I pick? I suppose Pizza Face and Tiny are just as good as Fat Boy and Hairball.

I remind myself that I really should be nice to Tiny

because she actually does well in school. Now that we're on the same team, maybe I can copy some notes for some other classes.

"Libby, this is Sheldon." Tiny introduces me to Pizza Face as we head down to the parking lot.

He opens his mouth, but nothing comes out.

"You're going to have to use your outdoor voice," I say, "because I can't hear you."

"It's nice to meet you," Sheldon says, a little louder this time.

"Libby and I go to school together, Shel. She's the one who came up with the Speak-Like-a-Poet Day I told you about."

Sheldon nods. I think he's saying something, because his mouth is open again, but then again, maybe he's just yawning.

So I yawn too.

As I get into my car, I see Tiny get into Pizza Face Sheldon's car.

He glares at me. But Tiny smiles and means it as she tells me to have a nice weekend.

15.

I'm sitting with Kenji drinking a beer at my Dead Celebrity Party. I am dressed up as Marilyn Monroe. Kenji is dressed up as Fat Elvis. Sid comes as Kurt Cobain. Perla arrives as Madonna.

"Perla, Madonna's not *dead*," I say.

"This is Madonna as the Material Girl, you know, circa 1985. That Madonna *is* dead," she says.

"Whatever," I say.

As usual there are more boys at the party than girls.

After a couple of beers, I'm drunk, so I look around for Kenji. I want to make out.

"Libby, you throw such a *great* party," Perla says, putting her arm around me. Her lipstick is smeared, and Mike Dutko comes out of the guest room behind her, zipping up his pants.

"Ugh, Mike Dutko?" I say. "Again?"

"Well, you know, boys are only good for one thing." Perla shrugs.

"What's that?" Sid says as he kind of sneaks up behind us, trying to join our conversation.

Sid's the only guy at the party who hasn't been hooking up.

"Bonehead," Perla says. Sid ignores her.

Then she kind of looks him up and down, like she isn't seeing anything worth her time. But she can't help it, I notice; her eyes linger a second too long on his crotch.

Mike Dutko comes over to join us again. He's brought Perla a drink. He can't get enough of her. He slips his hand around her waist, and she smiles and leads him back into the guest room. Perla's not against going back for seconds.

"What an idiot," I say.

"Do you mean Mike Dutko?" Sid asks. "Or me?"

"I don't know," I answer. "Both of you. And Perla." Sid laughs.

"I bet the L.A. Zoo is pretty cool as far as internships go," Sid says. "I wish I had the time to do an internship."

"It's not brain surgery," I say. "You could do it."

"I don't have the time. I'm on scholarship. I have an after-school job."

"Oh, yeah," I say. Sid is a receptionist at a hair salon. At least he gives discounts. And his hair always looks good.

"Do you get to see the condors?"

"No. No one gets to see the condors."

"That's a bummer. Once a couple of years ago, my parents and I were camping, and we saw a condor. I knew it was a condor 'cause my dad had a field guide to birds 'cause he likes to bird watch."

I don't say anything. I just watch as Kenji's eyes zoom in on the two of us. He's smooth-talking some girls on the other side of the room.

I can smooth-talk too. I lean in close to Sid, hoping Kenji will notice. I want him to feel as jealous as I do.

"Oh, we have to do like a field guide," I say. "Like observe the animals every minute. Take notes on their behavior. We can tell how the animals are doing by what they're doing."

I know that I am having an effect on Sid, because he licks his lips, and I can see his Adam's apple move up and down as he swallows.

"What language are you two speaking? Geek?" Kenji says. He's joined us, like I hoped he would.

"No," Sid says. "Smart."

Kenji snorts so hard that I think I see beer come out of his nose before he sucks it back in.

"Sid, I gotta ask you. Are you making a move on Libby?" Kenji asks. "I mean, 'cause I don't think I've ever seen you make a move."

"No," Sid says. "I'm not making a move."

He retreats a step and pulls the hood of his sweatshirt up over his head.

" 'Cause I, for one, would be curious as to what a Sid move would look like." Kenji laughs.

"Ha, ha," Sid says.

"Would you dazzle a lady with your weird philosophies?

Would you bore her with your encyclopedic musical brain? Or would you just grab her boobs?"

Kenji grabs at my chest.

"Cut it out," I say, wiggling away.

"I think I'll go and change the music," Sid says.

"You go do that," Kenji says. "Just don't put your fucking band demo on. It's not rock enough. It's like girly-boy music."

Kenji gropes me and starts kissing my neck.

"I just got an idea for a new song," Sid says. "It's called 'A Mountain of Asshole Stands Before Me in B-flat.'"

"Better run along and write it down then," Kenji says.

Sid moves off toward the computer and starts futzing with the iTunes playlist.

"I think you hurt his feelings," I say.

"No. He's hypersensitive. You know, *artistic*. I'm doing him a favor. I'm making his skin thicker."

Kenji pulls me close. His tongue licks my lips and runs along my teeth until I'm all hot and bothered. I pull him into a quiet corner.

"You're my girl," he whispers, his tongue flicking in my ear. Making my skin tingle. His arms coil around me.

"Snake," I say. "Tonight you're my snake."

16.

"So, Libby," Mom says, hanging up the phone. "That was Perla's mother. Evidently Perla came home drunk Saturday night after attending a party at our house."

"Mmm-hmm," I say.

"Did you have a party while your father and I were in Desert Hot Springs?"

"Uhm. I can't remember. What exactly did we agree was the definition of a party?"

"More than fifteen people."

"It wasn't a party then. It was a get-together."

"Were you drinking?" Mom asks.

"There might have been some beer. I can't remember."

"Well, I guess you're grounded, then."

"Okay," I say.

I whip out my cell phone and start to call Perla.

"What are you doing?" Mom asks.

"Just 'cause I'm grounded doesn't mean I can't run out and get a coffee, right?"

"I mean it this time," Mom says.

Yeah, right. I sigh and hang up my cell phone.

Dad passes me in the hall and picks up his keys off the hook.

"Where are you going?" I ask.

"Grocery store," he says.

"Can I come?"

"Okay," he says.

"Libby's grounded, Mitch," Mom says. "She had a party this weekend."

"Okay," he says. "Then I guess I'll drive."

"Hopeless," she mutters as she throws her arms up in the air. I grab my sweater.

It's the same old routine. Even when my mom means it, she doesn't *really* mean it.

17.

Dad and I have the Thanksgiving-is-next-week shopping list. I push the cart. I remember when that used to be fun, after I was too big to stand in the cart, like the captain of a ship, pulling products off the shelves as Dad read the list in a booming voice, calling foods by antique and archaic names: victuals, comestibles, viands, legumes, verdure, herbage.

Tonight he grunts one-word answers to my questions, and his mouth hangs downward in a perma-frown. Food shopping is a long way from being fun now.

For a while we walk side by side in silence. When we pass a product that he worked on a campaign for, he blows his lips out, like a horse. It is an unspoken rule that once he's worked on a product's ad campaign, we never buy that product again. We leave it on the shelf and buy the competition.

"Mitchell?" A man says to my dad.

He's a Hollywood hipster type. Vintage Levi's, tan skin, probably a bit of Botox. He looks familiar.

"Neil," Dad says.

The two men shake hands.

"God, it's good to see you," Neil says, glancing at me. "Is this Libby?"

I nod.

"Last time I saw you, you were just learning how to walk," Neil says.

"It worked out," I say. "I'm pretty good at it now."

Finally I realize that I've seen him in a few movies and TV shows.

"What are you up to?" Neil turns to my dad.

"Oh, this and that," my dad says. "You know how it is."

He looks uncomfortable. He loosens his tie.

"Your dad was one of the best writers I ever knew in the scene," Neil says.

"Really?" I say.

"Did you ever finish that Great American Play?" Neil asks.

"I got into advertising instead."

Dad says it all quiet, like it's a bad thing. Like he's embarrassed.

"Ah."

There's a long pause.

"You've been doing well. I caught your last film on cable the other night," Dad finally says.

"Yeah. Things seem to be going great," Neil says.

He knocks wood on his head three times.

"That's great," Dad says.

"Great," I say, almost under my breath.

"Well, good seeing you, Neil," Dad says, and we start to move along.

Dad picks up the signal I was sending him. He's good like that.

"Yeah, you too," Neil says.

They shake hands.

"Oh, hey! Mitchell!" Neil suddenly exclaims, turning back down the aisle toward us. "A group of us have a theater company going again. Just to, you know, get away from Hollywood. Jake's there. And Eddie's running it; he's clean and sober now. We just missed the old days, you know?"

"Yeah," Dad says. "I do."

Then they start talking about the old days and the Alphaville Theater, the collective that I discover Dad and Neil helped start in college. Pretty much everyone they mention is a successful actor or director now.

"You were going to be a revolutionary writer," Neil says. "What happened, man?"

I have never seen Dad's face look so alive. Talking to Neil, he looks like a young man. All his worry lines turn into laugh lines.

"I got sidetracked," Dad says. And I notice that he glances in my direction.

It hits me. He got sidetracked. By *me*.

"I'm having a baby," Neil says. "It's about time I became a dad. You know what they say nowadays, life begins after forty."

"Yeah," Dad says. "Life begins after forty."

"Well, here's my card. Call me. We'll go for a beer or something. You can come by the house. I'll show you my cars."

"Okay," my dad says.

Neil pulls a bottle of gourmet salsa off the shelf and disappears down the aisle.

Dad doesn't say anything for two aisles, and then he stops. I keep rolling forward, struggling with the cart, until I notice he's not with me. I turn around.

Dad is standing in the middle of the soup aisle. He looks confused.

No.

He looks *lost.*

18.

Perla leans over to check her face in the side mirror of my car.

"Oh, my God," she says.

"What?" I say, jumping off the hood and joining her by the door.

I turn around in time to see Tiny Carpentieri walking toward us.

Kenji elbows Perla in the rib cage, and they begin to laugh.

"Hi, Tina." Sid says

"Hi, Sid," she says. "Hi, Libby."

I look down at her. Way down.

"Yes?" I ask.

"Well, I was wondering if I could get a ride with you

the day after tomorrow to pick up our zoo shirts. Sheldon has a prior engagement."

"You don't have a car?"

"No."

"Then how do you get around?" I ask.

"I take the bus. Or I bum rides off of people."

"The bus?" I laugh.

"*No one* takes the bus in Los Angeles," Kenji says.

"I take the bus," Sid says.

Kenji laughs out loud. "Of course *you* take the bus, Sid."

"Libby, come on! We got stuff to *do*," Perla yells from the passenger seat, her bare feet sticking out the open window. Her toenails are painted pink with white daisies on them.

"I'll meet you here at the flagpole at 2:45."

"Thanks," Tiny says, smiling widely. She waves goodbye and leaves.

"I bet she can't drive 'cause she can't reach the pedals," Kenji says.

"I can't believe you have to work with her now, Libby. She looks like some kind of freaky *doll*." Perla laughs.

"She looks nothing like a *doll*," I say.

"Yeah, maybe it's more like an action figure," Mike Dutko says.

Kenji high-fives him.

"Tina is not a joke," Sid says.

"What is she, like, your girlfriend?" Kenji says.

Sid doesn't answer.

"You *love* her," Perla teases. She starts clapping. "Sid loves Tiny."

"You guys are being total assholes," Sid says.

"Come on, Perla, get out of the car," I say. "Kenji. Let's go be alone."

Kenji puts on a smug face as he trades places in the passenger seat with Perla. I drive quickly, eager for a distraction.

19.

Kenji and I are lying on his bed watching a DVD I didn't want to rent.

He starts kissing me. I feel nothing.

"Where are you?" he asks.

"What do you mean?" I say.

"Aren't you into it?"

"I guess," I say.

"You guess?"

"Well, sometimes hanging out feels *too* easy. You know?"

"No, because you hold out on me all the time," he says. "Maybe I should go out with Perla. Did you ever notice she's a *hand talker?*"

"No," I say.

"You know," he says. He puts his fist in front of his crotch and mocks a hand job. "She's like the Hand Job Queen."

I give him a look.

"You're disgusting," I say.

He laughs and pulls me in for a kiss.

"I wish you were going to be available during the winter break and around after school and stuff," he says.

"Just 'cause I have this zoo internship doesn't mean I'm not available," I say.

"Well, you can't come to Disneyland with us. I mean it's Junior Cut Day. It's a tradition," he says.

"I have to go pick up my zoo uniform and get field observation training."

"See? It hasn't even started yet and it's already cramping your style."

"Oh, please," I say. "Once you've seen the Disney Christmas parade, you've seen it."

He pulls me in for another kiss. I hold back my tongue.

"Do you want to do it?" he asks, all low-like, trying to sound sexy.

"No," I say.

But I let him put his hand down my pants.

20.

Tiny is by the flagpole at 2:45.

The Santa Ana winds are blowing hard, and it looks like it takes an effort for her to keep her feet on the ground.

She waves and starts walking over to me.

"This way, my car is this way," I say, forcing her back to the flagpole and into the parking lot. I don't really want to be seen with her.

We get into the car, and she pulls a triangular thing out of her backpack. She attaches it to the seat belt.

"What are you doing?"

"I'm too small for the belt. It's a child belt adjuster," she says. "By the way, can you turn this air bag off? It's dangerous for small children and Little People; see, it says so right here."

"No, I can't."

"Why not?"

"'Cause, I don't know how."

"Well, drive carefully then," Tiny says.

I set the car in drive and head toward the zoo.

Then Tiny starts humming. Could she *be* more annoying?

*   *   *

"Do you have an extra-small?" Tiny asks the zoo volunteer coordinator in charge of handing out the shirts.

"One size fits all," he replies.

"Good thing I know how to sew," Tiny informs him. "I'm on stage crew, and sometimes I have to help out with the costumes."

"Mmm-hmm," he says.

Why does she have to overexplain everything?

"Looks like he's going to have a problem too." Tiny says, pointing to an extremely obese volunteer. It's Fat Boy, from orientation.

"Ready to go, Tiny?" I ask.

"It's *Tina*," Tiny says. "Hang on just a sec."

I watch as Tiny goes over to Fat Boy and says something to him. He starts to laugh. I see her hold up her shirt, then he holds up his shirt, which looks like it will be ten times too small.

She pats his arm, and she heads back toward me.

"What happened there?" I ask.

"I told Matthew that I'm going to alter my shirt to fit me, so I'll save the extra fabric and alter his too."

"I don't understand," I say.

"He's big. I'm small," Tiny says, like I'm slower than slow.

"No, I mean, why do that for him? You don't even know him," I say.

"Don't you ever do anything for someone just to help them out?"

"No," I say.

"Well, you should try it."

God. What does she want me to do? Like, good for her—she's a nice girl. I'm not.

"I don't care what that guy says. Look around, open your eyes," Tiny says. "One size does not fit all."

I really think about that for a minute.

"It must be a drag to adjust the world to fit you everywhere you go."

"No shit, Sherlock," Tiny says.

21.

"So then, by the teacups? Oh, my God! It was so funny," Perla says.

"What?" I ask.

It is very boring to listen to the blow-by-blow account of a day that you did not participate in, especially when Perla is telling the story while sitting on your bed, painting her toenails "do me" red and dripping nail polish everywhere.

Perla is not a good storyteller.

"Hysterical!" she says. "Then Mike Dutko is like running alongside the parade, declaring his true love to Snow White, and she's like looking at him like he's crazy. And then we did the Tower of Terror like three times; I totally threw up, but Sid didn't want to go the third time. He was like spouting some shit about something. So he just watched our bags."

"That was nice of him," I say.

"Whatever."

If she had her laptop on, I'm sure she would show me the slide show of digital pictures of Disneyland to complement all the boring stories she's told me.

"I could totally be a better Snow White than the girl they had playing her. I'm prettier too. Then again, why would I want to play a character when I play a way better me?"

"Who else was there?" I ask.

"Oh, everyone. So it was so fun. Everyone was there," she says. "I mean, except you. I kind of hung out with Mike Dutko 'cause he keeps telling me he loves me. So, I might like him. Do you like him?"

"He's all right," I say.

"You're lucky. You have Kenji."

"Yeah," I say. "But I bet that Kenji was slithering around the pretty girls at the park."

"You know it," she says. "Men are such snakes. All they care about is . . ."

Perla takes her finger and sticks it repeatedly into the hole she makes with her other hand. The universal hand sign for Fucking. Then, trying to keep her toes unsmeared, she hobbles over to the TV in my room and turns it on. We start watching one of her dad's reality TV shows.

"When I get my show, *Ma Vida Loca,* I hope I get a killer time slot. I'm *so* prime time."

I'm supposed to like Perla's dad's show, but I can't concentrate. I am barely able to keep my eyes open on the bed while pretending to watch it, while Perla sits next to me, transfixed and laughing hysterically.

Right before I nod off, I realize that she hasn't asked me a single question about my day at the zoo.

22.

I'm on my way out to meet everyone at the movies.

"Dad, I need some money," I say.

Dad purses his lips.

"What happened to the money I gave you last time?" he asks.

"I spent it," I say.

Duh.

"Things are going to be different around here," Dad says.

He puts two twenties in my hand.

"Make it last," he adds.

I stamp my foot on the ground and storm out the door.

If they are going to charge a million dollars for a movie ticket, I look at it as an entry fee. Like to an amusement park.

The rules are simple. Procure ticket to movie. See movie. Go to bathroom one by one. Emerge once the previews start. See another movie. Repeat until bored or all movies in multiplex have been viewed.

Never make noise or giggle, or you will get kicked out. Wear beige. Do not buy popcorn or soda. Bring some snacks and soda pop in your backpack.

After coming out of our second film of the day, I hear laughing on the other side of the lobby. That's when I see Tiny and her friends. Two of them are acting out a scene from the movie we just saw. Tiny is standing up on the cushioned bench directing them. They don't get it right, but she doesn't get angry. She just hops off the bench and replaces one of her friends and shows them how the scene is done, complete with exaggerated death scene.

Even from this side of the room, I can hear Tiny's voice, a perfect mimic. Even from this side of the room, I crack a smile.

Perla rolls her eyes.

"Dorks," she says.

All of their kind of fun is sadly way over Perla's head. And so we resort to doing what we always do: standing around and hating everything.

Kenji and Mike Dutko emerge from the action flick that they saw. Kenji shakes his hair out of his eyes. He zips up his jacket and flicks his chin out toward me to say hello.

"Back to school tomorrow," Perla says.

"Yep, back to school," I say.

Then Perla pretends to stick her finger down her throat and throw up.

23.

Sheldon is wearing a flannel shirt and an old-man sweater. I'm fixated on the bad fashion choice.

"Hello," he says.

His voice is so quiet it's barely above a whisper. "Hello," I say.

"Okay, Blue Team!" Tiny says, waving our first assignment sheets as she practically skips over to us. "Today we're observing spider monkeys!"

I take a step forward, and my platform heel catches on a little bump in the pavement. I stumble.

"Guess these aren't the greatest walking shoes," I say.

"No shit?" Tiny says, laughing.

She and Sheldon pause for a second to make sure I'm all right, then they keep moving till we get to the monkey cage.

"I don't know what we're looking for," I say.

"Spider monkeys," Tiny says. "Today we're collecting data."

I already have a blister from walking, so I sit down on a bench. Without a word, Sheldon hands me the Blue Team field notebook and a pen.

"Male spider monkey eats celery," he says.

"What?"

"Write it down," Tiny says. Then she makes another observation: "Male swings from tree."

"Female rests on branch," Sheldon says. I have to strain to hear him. "Write it down," he urges me.

"Young swings to adult female," Tiny says. "Don't

forget, Libby—you have to enter the time the action happened."

I don't tell her that I'm not wearing a watch today. I didn't have one that matched my outfit.

I pick up the pen and start writing the data that Tiny and Sheldon quickly feed me. My hand cramps. It's hard to keep up. I fake half of it.

Personally, I don't notice a single thing.

When I get home, I sit in my car in the driveway for a while, leaning my head on my furry steering wheel.

I'm useless.

24.

End of fall semester grades:
English: B
History: B–
Math: B
Biology: B–
Art: B+

"We pay a lot for that school," Dad says.

"I just think you have to try harder," Mom says,

examining my report card. "Though, I am encouraged by this zoo internship you're taking."

"When does that start?" Dad asks.

"It started today," I say. "And since when is a B bad?" I ask.

"It's mediocre," Dad says.

"It's a B," I say. "Bs are good."

"But we know you're not working at it," Mom says.

"You said you got Bs in high school, Mom, and it was like the greatest thing ever," I say.

"I worked hard for those Bs. I am not as smart as you are. You could be an A student," Mom says.

"Why?" I say. "Why do I have to?"

"Because you are a smart girl," Dad says.

"Because you'll want to get into a good college," Mom says.

"Why bother?" I say. "There are no jobs. The economy sucks. Everybody hates the U.S. I mean, they are trying to *kill* us."

"That's no reason not to try, Libby," Mom says. "That's no reason to jeopardize your future."

"You're a smart girl, Libby. You can do anything you want," Dad says. "But one day you're not just going to be able to coast by."

Wanna bet?

57

25.

I am sitting in the café with my boys, Kenji, Mike Dutko, and Sid. Kenji is sitting next to me. He smells like lemon.

I want to be close to someone. I put my arm around Kenji. He slides in closer to me.

"So, how was the internship?" Sid asks. "Didn't that start today?"

I don't want to talk about it. I don't want to say that I wore the wrong shoes, stepped in a pile of shit, got lost trying to find the zoo exit.

"It was like being exiled to the Siberia of social rejects," I say. "Mostly, so far, I've seen monkeys rub themselves."

"Hot," Mike Dutko says.

"Not so much," I say.

"I can't believe you haven't quit yet," Kenji says as he rubs my leg under the table.

"Yeah," Mike Dutko says, agreeing with Kenji as always.

"I think that's too bad," Sid says. "I thought it'd be different."

"Well, it's not," I say.

But it is different. And I don't think I like that.

I've finally come to the conclusion that all my friends might be right.

Maybe this internship *is* a bad idea.

26.

"Blue Team, today we're on elephant duty," Tiny says, joining us. Clearly, Tiny has assigned herself to be our team leader.

Toby, the animal services guy, has already moved the elephants inside so that it's safe for us to walk around the pens. We undo the padlock and begin bringing out the hay.

"Elephants are intelligent mammals," Toby explains. "One of our most important responsibilities here at the zoo is animal enrichment. That means we come up with new ways to keep them stimulated."

"How do you keep an elephant stimulated?" I say.

Tiny laughs. "Ew! That sounds dirty," she says.

"Yeah! I'm perverted," I say, and I laugh along with her.

"What's your name?" Toby asks.

"Libby."

"Libby, this is serious business. These animals are wild animals, and I expect you to be serious when you are working."

"Okay. I got it."

Sheldon says something.

"What?" I say, throwing my hands around like fake sign language. "I can't hear you."

Sheldon stares at me blankly.

"He said that we have to make sure that the mud pit is muddy enough," Tiny translates. "They love mud."

"That's correct," Toby says. "Good work, Sheldon and Tina. They also like bark. We need to make sure the bark is rough enough. That is something we check every day."

"How does Sheldon know that?" I ask.

"Duh, it's the example in the handbook they gave us at orientation," Tiny says.

"It's important that you read the handbook. That way you'll know to do things properly and safely," Toby says. Then he leaves us alone with a list of instructions.

Tiny shuffles through the hay toward Sheldon and begins to help as he hands me the field notebook. He doesn't have to say anything that I can't hear. I know what it means. It means stay out of the way, take down notations of what we've done, and watch the elephants and see what they do while Toby exercises them in their individual pens.

I know my place.

I'm the Blue Team pencil pusher.

This time, I try not to fall behind. I make an effort to pay attention. I note everything and I write fast. I list all the fruits and veggies that are in the food barrel. I even note how the elephants behave as Toby runs them through their muscle exercises.

3:46 Baby elephant stands up.

3:49 Baby elephant lies down.

3:52 Adult male elephant sits up.

3:54 Adult female elephant presents front feet on rail for scrubbing and trimming.

3:58 Adult female elephant puts rear feet on rail for cleaning.

Tiny and Sheldon seem to have all the hard stuff under control, the actual cleaning of the pens and the portioning out of the bale of hay. It's probably better this way. There might be big elephant turds everywhere, and I don't want to get dirty.

Toby keeps an eye on us from the pen he's in as he goes about his business. Occasionally he comes over to give us an additional duty to perform or to check on our progress.

"This place is a real shit hole," I say.

"You know what Toby said?" Sheldon says softly. "Elephants like to roam, and it's too small in the pens for them. So every other morning, they get walked once around the zoo."

"Hey, Toby!" Tiny yells out. Big voice. Little girl. "Can we come see the elephants roam one morning?"

How can Tiny hear Sheldon from where she is on the other side of the pen? I can barely hear him and he's working right next to me. Maybe because she got gypped in her body, she's got like bionic ears or something.

"Let's see how good a job you do," Toby says. "Now just concentrate on getting those pens ready so I can move the elephants back in there."

27.

Mom and Dad come out of the kitchen when they hear me walking down the hallway.

"Libby, where are you going?" Mom asks.

"Out," I say. I indicate my coat. "Duh."

"We need to talk to you," Dad says. "We need to have a family meeting."

"What is it?" I say.

"It's going to be a pretty low-key Christmas this year," Dad says.

"Okay, whatever," I say, and start to head out the door, my hand extended, waiting for the slap and slip of green. Only this time, Dad puts his hand into mine and looks at me.

"Things are going to be different around here," he says, "because I've quit my job."

He's obviously excited, and Mom is obviously not. She bites her lip and looks at the floor.

"Okay," I say, "but I'm still going out."

"Good, I'm glad you're all right with it," Dad says.

Then he heads back down the hall, kind of skipping. Mom turns her attention back to me, following me down the hallway to the front door.

"So, as Dad was saying, Christmas is going to be low-key. Pick one gift you really want. Something that's not *too* expensive," she says. "After all, the holidays aren't about presents. They're about us all being together, right?"

"Yeah, well, I already have plans during break, like, every day," I say.

Before she can respond, I'm out the door.

It's open mic night at the café, and Sid has signed up to play a song. We watch him from our table in the back as he mingles with the other musicians.

"I don't know why he always wears that sorry-ass green hoodie. And look, he cut the label off his jeans. Why?" Kenji says.

"I don't think he likes brands," I say. "Didn't he say that once?"

"Why does he always have to be so different?" Kenji says, then drains his cup of coffee. "Refill."

Kenji slides over to the coffee bar. On the way, he stops by the table of musicians where Sid is engaged in a serious conversation. Kenji slaps Sid on the back and slips himself between Sid and the guy he's talking to.

"Speaking of brands," Perla says, pushing the ice around in her Italian soda with a long spoon, "I want to get one of those T-shirts that has every single cool brand on it, like, in a pattern. Everybody wants it. I told my mom that's what I wanted for Christmas. It's, like, crazy expensive. You should get one too, Libby—then we can match. My dad told me it's going to be in the Paramount Studio Christmas gift bags."

"I don't want it," I say.

"Of course you do," Perla says. "It's *ironic.*"

"I don't want to match," I say, even though we are wearing the exact same outfit this evening. Baby pink T-shirts, arm warmers, low-slung button-up jeans, and boots.

28.

I am scattering straw down in the petting zoo. The pen is full of children and sheep and goats. One of the animal services guys is playing with a goat by bumping his forehead with it. The goat likes it. That's how they play; they bonk each other's heads.

I eye Sheldon, who is wearing another fashion disaster (high-waisted jeans, acid wash, too short, no belt, makes his butt look like a woman's), and I realize that he has said exactly three sentences to me today.

All this not talking is driving me crazy. The silence may actually kill me.

I stop with the working and start with the talking.

"So, what's your deal?" I ask Sheldon.

"What do you mean?" he asks.

"For starters, you don't go to our school," I say. "Where do you go?"

"I go to the Science Magnet," he says.

"Ew. Public school? Why?"

"I want to be an exobiologist."

"Exobiology?" I say. "Wha?"

"It's the study of alien life," he says.

"What does that mean?" I laugh.

Sheldon looks at me like I'm stupid.

"I mean, sorry, but there are no aliens."

"Don't be so sure," Sheldon says. "A lot of scientists think that life is rare. That Earth is rare. But I know there is more life out there. We can't be alone."

His face turns upward. My eyes follow his, but there is nothing up there to see but the smog that makes the sky look paper white today.

"Why do you work at the zoo, then?" I ask. "If you want to be an astronaut, or whatever, why don't you work at the Griffith Park Observatory?"

"They don't have internships," Sheldon says.

"Well, how about that NASA place?" I suggest.

"I don't do well at interviews," he says.

"You just need to stop whispering and speak up," I say. But even after it comes out of my mouth, I realize that it's kind of mean.

"The Jet Propulsion Laboratory is *very competitive*," Sheldon says. His hand movements become more animated as he tries to stress this point to me.

"But how could you not get in?" I ask. "Aren't you like a genius?"

He turns his usual shade of red as his blush creeps up all the way from his neck to his ears.

"Uh," he continues, ignoring my compliment, "so as an exobiologist, I want to see how animals adapt and are different on this planet so I can think about how they might live on other planets. I get an opportunity to do that here at the zoo."

Sheldon looks at his now still hands. The red in his face has retreated to a pale white. I bet he uses a lot of sunscreen on that sensitive skin of his. He seems relieved when Tiny appears so that he can change the subject.

"Tina, there's going to be a lunar eclipse at the end of the month," he says.

"Did you know you can go up to the observatory and they let you look through the big telescope?" Tiny says. "It's amazing. You can see the ice caps on Mars and the rings on Saturn."

"You don't need the observatory for that," Sheldon says. "I can see those things with my telescope at home."

I laugh. "Most boys have a telescope because they are perverts," I say. "Kenji totally told his parents he wanted to *stargaze,* but he really wanted a view of the girl who stars on that WB show who lives across the street from him. She walks around naked in her house all the time."

"N-n-n-o, I have a telescope because I want to be an *exobiologist* and I like to observe the night sky and— and dream about what might be out there," he stammers. He's turning all red again. "And I plan on being on one of the Mars teams one day."

Hey, Sheldon, I think. Try figuring out how to live on THIS planet.

29.

Perla and I are sitting in the tent, flipping through magazines by the light of her Hello Kitty lantern. We've been having sleepovers in the backyard since we were twelve. That way her parents can't eavesdrop on us.

We hear howling outside, quickly followed by laughing, which means the boys are here.

"Oh, please," I say through the fabric of the tent. "That was the worst animal call ever."

"Well, you would know. You work at the zoo," Perla says. "I myself am scared it might be rabid coyotes."

A hand starts to unzip the flap, and Kenji pokes his head inside.

"Yeah, you're right, Perla. It *is* rabid coyotes," I say.

"Are you ladies decent?" Kenji asks.

"Never," I say.

He climbs inside the tent, followed by Mike Dutko, who is holding a six-pack of beer.

"I thought Sid was coming too," Perla says.

"He'd just be a fifth wheel," Kenji says. "If you

know what I mean." He crawls across the sleeping bags and flops his head on my lap. I know what he wants. I want it too.

"Come on," I say, taking his hand. "Let's go find some privacy."

I pick up one of the sleeping bags and lead Kenji outside, leaving Mike Dutko and Perla wrestling each other out of their clothing inside the tent.

We spread the sleeping bag on the ground, and Kenji pulls me on top of him.

"Oh, yeah," he says as I start kissing him and sliding my hands under his shirt. His chest is smooth. His skin warms my hands. We roll around for a little while, and when I find myself underneath him, I open my eyes and look up at the stars.

"What are you doing?" Kenji murmurs. "Don't stop."

"Do you think there is life on other planets?" I ask.

"What?" he says. He starts to unbutton my jeans. But he cannot distract me from the universe stretched out above me.

"Life on other planets. I mean look at all those stars."

Kenji gives up. He sighs, then rolls onto his back and looks up at the sky with me.

"Yeah, I guess, maybe there's something out there," he says, then adds in an alien voice, *We are not alone.*"

"Did you ever wonder what they might look like?"

"No," he says.

"Did you know that there are people whose job it is to think about what they might look like?"

"No shit?"

We lie there for a while, my head on his chest. He puts his arm around me as he relaxes into looking up at the night sky.

Then his cell phone rings. I feel his voice through his chest as he speaks.

"Hey, there's a party over at Jakob's. You want to head over there?"

I look back over at the tent, which is now dark.

"I have to be at the zoo at eight-thirty tomorrow morning."

"It's *vacation week*," Kenji says. "Don't be a pussy."

"Okay," I say.

I don't really want to go to Jakob's, knowing that I'll crawl home at the crack of dawn and the zoo will smell even worse with a hangover. But I don't want to be a pussy.

"I'll go, but I won't really drink," I add.

"Good, then you can drive."

Jakob's house is a scene. The mash-up music, bass turned up to ten, shakes me down to my bones. As soon as we get there, I already want to leave. Maybe even run. I don't care where or what direction.

"I'll go get us drinks," Kenji says, and he makes his way down the crowded hallway, saying hellos to everybody who's anybody.

There are so many people that I feel like I am being squeezed. I make my way over to the couch that has been cleared from the center of the living room to make room for dancing.

If Perla were here, I might go over there and dirty dance. Instead, I sit on the couch next to a couple that is making out.

Kenji finds me and presses a soda into my hand.

"This is great!" he says. "I'm going to go out back to play darts."

"Okay," I say. The can is sweaty. I start playing with the pull tab.

He kisses me and then disappears again. *He* is having fun. Everyone's having fun. So I force myself to stay.

I turn my attention back to the scenes playing out in front of me. I'm in observation mode.

2:05 a.m. Girls, half dressed, half drunk, writhing like they are in some kind of harem. They reach out, trying to entice observer to dance.

2:14 Guy on couch throws one leg over

	girl he is kissing, trying to rub her as much as he can.
2:34	Bunch of guys gathers around alpha male in the corner. Safety in numbers.
2:37	Alpha male chugs beer.
3:01	Girl and guy leave couch and enter bedroom.
3:23	While obtaining glass of water, observer discovers puke in kitchen sink.
4:12	Second wave of kids arrives from other party.

I leave the party at six a.m but instead of heading home, I go to Fred 62 and get myself some breakfast. Then I head to the zoo.

I need something new to observe.

I walk up to the main gate. The zoo is closed, and no one is around. I head over to the employee-only entrance, but before I get there, a security guard drives up in his little golf cart.

"Can I help you, Miss?" he asks.

"I volunteer at the zoo," I say.

"Zoo's closed now," he says.

I fumble in my wallet and show him my L.A. Zoo Volunteer ID.

"I was wondering if I could see the elephants. Toby said they walk them at around seven a.m."

The security guard looks at my ID, then takes his walkie-talkie from his belt loop and talks into it. He gets a garbled response.

"Okay." He looks at me. "Hop in. I'll take you up there."

Toby meets me outside the elephant pens.

"Libby. Well, *this* is a surprise."

He looks at me the same way that I see him looking at the elephants when he's inspecting them from behind the safety guard. He doesn't seem to find anything wrong with me.

"Just stay out of the way," he tells me as he leads out the elephants. One follows the other, just as I follow Toby. The elephants walk steadily and slowly, heads bobbing up and down, as we pass the other animals. It's as though they're saying good morning.

I feel small next to their gray greatness.

30.

Later that day, Sheldon, Tiny, and I are standing in line to have our pictures taken with the reindeer and Santa Claus at the zoo. We are done working for the day, and Tiny thought it might be fun, since this is the day before the day before Christmas.

"This is retarded," I say.

I am trying to be a good Blue Team member, but the lack of sleep and superearly arrival at the zoo make it painful.

"How is this more retarded than Pencil Day?" Tiny asks. "And by the way, you shouldn't use the word *retarded.*"

"*I* came up with Pencil Day," I say. "And it certainly didn't involve kids pissing their pants everywhere."

"What's Pencil Day?" Sheldon asks, but we don't answer because a kid in line behind us starts pointing and yelling.

"Mommy, look! A real elf!" the kid says.

The smile on Tiny's face disappears. Sheldon becomes very stiff, and the red creeps up his neck and onto his face. The kid is pointing at Tiny.

"I want to meet the elf! I want to meet the elf!" the kid yells.

At first, no one does anything, not even the mom. Everyone just stands around awkwardly, pretending they can't hear him. Everyone except me. I lean down so I'm face to face with the kid.

"*Those* are the elves," I say, pointing to the people in the elf costumes taking pictures of the kids with Santa and his reindeer.

"She's a *person*," I inform the kid, pointing at Tiny.

"Oh," he says. He now points over in the right area. "Those are the elves."

"You made a mistake," I say.

"Mommy, Mommy, I want to meet the elves!" he shouts, tugging at her sleeve.

"I'm sorry," the mom says to Tiny.

"Happens all the time," Tiny says, like it doesn't matter. She's used to it. But I can tell that it bothers her.

I have a big mouth, and today I have no patience, and although Tiny probably always just lets it slide, I can't. It bothers *me*.

"You're an asshole for letting your kid say that," I say.

Now the mom's hands slip over her kid's ears. She apologizes again. She's upset now. Good. She leans down to her kid, and I hear her finally doing her job, explaining about how there are different types of people in the world.

"You don't need to speak for me, you know," Tiny says. "I can take care of myself."

I don't know what to say.

Finally, it's our turn to go through the gate. I can see that the holiday spirit has fled from the typically perky Tiny. The fun has been sucked right out of her. I know what I need to do.

"Come on, Blue Team! I declare it Reindeer Day!" I say.

I pull one of the reindeer headbands from the costume peg, put it on my head, and strike a reindeer pose.

Sheldon steers Tiny through the gate, and they take some reindeer antlers and put them on their heads as well.

We gather around Santa and the real reindeer and start to pose when I get another idea.

"Wait! Hold the picture!" I say. I grab my bag and dig around until I pull out my fire-engine red lipstick and a mirror. I smear red all over my nose.

I hear the kids in the line get all excited. They jump up and down.

"Look, Mommy," one kid starts yelling. "It's Rudolph!"

31.

The first order of business this Christmas morning is a heavy dose of caffeine. I know it's time to wake up when I hear the sound of the espresso machine.

"Merry Christmas!" Dad says.

I grunt in reply, sticking my arms out in front of me like a sleep zombie. He puts a mug of steaming latte in my hands.

"Go wake up your mom so we can eat breakfast and open presents," Dad says.

Christmas has always been Mom's favorite holiday. But this year Dad's the one with more spirit. He's flipping flapjacks and cooking eggs. He's got an apron on that says, *I'm the Frog Prince*. And I think he means it.

The latte begins working its caffeinated magic as I go to the kitchen door and lean my head around into the hallway.

"Mom!!!!!!! WAKE UP!!!!!!" I yell.

Dad laughs. He's just tickled pink by everything lately.

The yelling has done its trick. Mom makes her way into the kitchen to join us.

"Let's make this quick. I've got plans," I say.

"Where's your Christmas spirit, Libby?" Mom says, even though she barely has any herself this year.

"Let's just call her *The Grinch,*" Dad says. He still thinks he's being funny, even though Mom and I aren't laughing.

"Come on," Dad says, making the first move to the living room. He actually seems kind of excited as we all stare at the tree and the visibly-fewer-than-usual presents under it.

"I'll go first," I say, breaking the silence in the room. I give my parents their presents: Chinese slippers, a crepe pan, some tennis balls, and a tennis skirt for Mom. A leather wallet and zoo passes for Dad.

My stocking is stuffed with bath stuff, lipstick, an orange, some gum that looks like a lump of coal, and, as a joke, some of those low-carb chocolate bars Dad was writing about before he quit.

"Ha," I say.

"I had to get rid of them," Dad says. "They were bringing me down."

"I'll give them to Perla. She's always on a diet."

I start unwrapping the packages under the tree. I get a sweater that I hate, a new hair dryer, a pair of silk pajamas that I wanted but in the wrong color (typical), and gift certificates to Amoeba Music, Fred Segal, and Sephora.

At least my parents have learned to let me make *some* decisions for myself.

Later, before I go to meet Sid and Mike Dutko for Chinese food and a movie, I hear my parents arguing in their room.

It seems as though there are more of these kinds of conversations behind closed doors lately. Why is it that parents think that shutting the door means that you can't hear them when they yell at each other? It may be muffled, but it's coming through loud and clear.

"I thought we agreed, Mitch, a *small* Christmas, no big presents. How could you get those gift certificates?" Mom yells. "You should have talked to me about it. We had an agreement."

"She's a teenager, Julietta," Dad says calmly. "I can't make her suffer because I'm changing my life."

"She may be the teenager, but *you're* the one acting like a kid. An irresponsible kid," Mom says. "I don't even know who you are anymore."

Her voice sounds weird. She might be crying.

"I'm the kid you fell in love with," Dad says, soothing.

"I don't want to lose everything," Mom says.

"Trust me," he says. And as long as he says it, with all that love, I know they're not heading for Splitsville.

A few minutes later, Mom and Dad come out of the

bedroom all dressed up to go out, wearing big smiles and acting as though nothing has happened at all.

"Do you want us to drop you off somewhere?" Dad asks.

"Yeah, I'm going to the movies," I say.

32.

As I emerge from the shed after putting away my brushes and carefully washing my hands, I see Sheldon standing in front of the giraffes.

He's stretching his neck, hopping slowly from side to side. At first I think he's doing tai chi or yoga or maybe just losing his mind. That wouldn't surprise me. Then I realize that he's trying to move his body like the giraffe.

What *would* it be like to be a giraffe? I wonder, slowing down. I stretch out my own neck and crane it toward the nearest bush. I open my mouth and pull off a leaf.

"What are you doing, weirdo?"

I spit the leaf out and look around. Sheldon is staring at me, and Tiny looks very amused.

"I was hungry," I say. "And the food here sucks."

"You already look like a giraffe," Tiny says. "Don't you think, Sheldon? With that ballerina neck of hers?"

"I always thought she moved like a gazelle," Sheldon says. "Very graceful. But she's definitely doe-eyed, like the giraffe."

"And her hair color is kind of the same shade as the giraffe," Tiny says. "Me, I'm slightly warthog-like, don't you think?"

"Why do you say that?" Sheldon says.

"Because of the way I walk," Tiny says.

"I always thought you were more koala-like."

"Ha!" she says, "You're just being generous."

"Boy," I say. "And you're calling *me* weirdo?"

"Hey," Tiny yells to me from across the parking lot.

"Hey," I yell back as I start to open my car door. But I'm not fast enough, and she and Sheldon catch up to me.

"We're going to go and have a little walk by the old zoo," Tiny says, a bit breathless. I think it's sometimes an effort for her to run. "Want to come?"

I want to say, no, I don't. I have plans for this afternoon. I have things to do. Like shop. It's the day after Christmas, and I have three gift certificates to spend. I can't be hanging out with you guys. I don't even really *like* you guys.

But it's already three p.m., and I bet that everything good is already gone, and I don't really want to go shopping by myself. So really I have nothing to do at all.

"Okay," I say.

"Terrific," Tiny says. "It's not far. Just follow us."

I get into my car and follow them deeper into Griffith Park. I want to go faster, but Sheldon insists on going the speed limit, twenty-five miles an hour. Finally we park. I get out of my car and look around. I see nothing but trees and picnic tables.

"Great," I say. "What a waste of time."

Sheldon rolls his eyes and mumbles something.

"I can't hear you," I say.

"He said, *follow me*," Tiny says. They start walking past the trees, past some picnic tables, and up some stairs. Soon, I see a row of impossibly small cages. There's a sign above them.

It's the Old Zoo.

Tiny sits on the grass under the shade of a large tree and opens her bag, pulling out three bottles of water, and hands one to Sheldon and one to me. She stares at the cages. Her face has a far-off look on it.

The cages are open. There are picnic tables inside them. I move toward the first one. I step inside. Immediately, it's claustrophobic. There is no room, and the fake rock face has no purpose. It's desolate, like an animal ghost town.

"How could this be a zoo?" I say. "How could they think that animals would be okay in these cages? What about the animal enrichment? And how did they roam?"

"They didn't," Sheldon says. He must be projecting because I can hear him fine.

"This place is depressing," I say. "I bet a lot of animals died of sadness here."

Tiny and Sheldon watch me as I pace inside, twenty steps one way and twenty steps the other.

"Or boredom," I add. "I bet they were totally bored."

33.

Perla is showing me all of the clothes she got for Christmas.

She is wearing that shirt that she wanted me to get. The brands run together like, maybe, an old cheeky Andy Warhol painting. Only I think the joke is on Perla, because when I stare at the shirt long enough I notice that the negative space between the logos spells out the words "BRAND WHORE." As she continues to pull clothes out of her color-coordinated closet, I decide to keep this discovery to myself.

But the more I look at all those brands, the more I want to cut them up.

"So, we don't even have a New Year's Eve plan," Perla says. "We always have a New Year's Eve plan by now."

"Don't worry—I've got it covered. I'm going to throw a party," I say.

"Oooh, perfect! Do you think your parents will let you?"

"Leave that to me," I say. "But here's the theme: Fashion Deconstruction."

"What's that?"

"I'm not sure yet. But that's what it's called."

"I love it!" Perla says. "I'll post it on my blog."

"Yeah, invite all real-life people. Let's make it huge."

"Everyone will come, Libby. Your parties are off the hook."

She bounces on the bed and hugs me.

34.

I run into Sheldon in the parking lot, and he waits for me to park my car, so I have to walk up to the zoo with him.

Lately, the wind must be blowing the words from

his mouth in my direction, because I can actually hear them. Too bad I can't understand most of them.

"I don't know what that means," I say after he throws out a fantastically-ginormous word.

He looks at me blank-faced.

"I don't know what that means," I say again.

"I know. *I* heard *you*. I just find that amazing," he says. "How are you ever going to handle taking the SATs next year?"

Sheldon seems to go out of his way to make me feel like an idiot. But then again, maybe I am an idiot. For not paying attention. For not making an effort.

"Well, I once heard a story about a guy who filled in his SAT score sheet to look like a duck, and he got into Yale."

"That's an urban myth," Sheldon says.

"No, it's not," I say. But actually, I can't remember exactly where or from whom I heard it.

"I'm not an academic like you and Tiny," I say.

"It's almost a new year. You could turn over a new leaf," he says in his careful way. "Or is that not cool enough? Would you rather keep pretending to be a dilettante?"

"Yeah, another word I'm not hanging on to," I say.

"I don't know why everyone thinks you're so cool," he says, shaking his head.

"Some people just are," I inform him. "And some just aren't."

I think he knows who I mean. But just in case, I look him up and down, taking in those acid wash women's jeans he's sporting again, then look over at Tiny, who is waiting for us by the zoo entrance, her little hands on her regular-size curvy hips.

"Today we're with the chimpanzees!" she yells.

"I think Tina is cool," Sheldon says.

"Well, you're a fan club of one," I say.

He wants to say more, but I think he's hit a wall. Thank God, he goes back to being quiet.

35.

"Libby! It's for you!" Mom yells to me.

"Hey, ho!" I say into the phone.

"Hey! I'm not a ho!"

"Tiny?"

"It's Tina," she says without missing a beat. "So, tonight's New Year's Eve, and you know, I'm just calling around to people I know to see what's going on. I know that the Science Club is having a party at Melvin's house, so I could do that. There's the LPA New Year's

Bash, which is usually a good time. And Sheldon has a date with his telescope to look at the night sky; that's always an option. But . . ."

"But what?" I ask.

Please don't invite yourself to my party. Please don't invite yourself to my party.

"I heard you were having a party, and I know your parties are legendary," she says.

"How do you know I'm having a party?" I ask.

"Well, I read Perla's blog. And since she said that all real-life people are invited, and I'm in your real life . . . I was wondering if you really meant it."

What does it mean when you really mean something, only you don't really mean it for everyone? Does that make you a liar?

"Why do you want to come to my party?"

"I thought it'd be a fun change," she says.

We're both quiet for a moment. Dad always says, when negotiating, never be the first person to speak. So it's a tug of war.

At last Tiny takes a deep breath and breaks the silence.

"Look, I'm just tired of hanging out with all the same people all the time."

Unfortunately, I know exactly how she feels.

★   ★   ★

I love drinking beer in the rec room.

My mom and dad bought the keg. That is the concession that they made to keep me from going out into the wild world of New Year's Eve. A keg is cheaper than the fake New Year's Eve plan I proposed, which involved an unchaperoned trip to Las Vegas. I have learned that the best way to get what I want is to propose something wildly out of the question to my parents. Then they always say yes to the much milder Plan B.

My mom comes into the room. She points at the pile of shredded clothes.

"What are you kids doing?" she asks. She picks up a frayed sleeve. "Isn't this the sweater I bought you for Christmas?"

"Mom. The theme is Fashion Deconstruction," I inform her. "You must put together an outfit if you are to come in here."

"Oh, Libby," Mom says. "You are so creative."

She rummages through the pile and pins a stray flower onto her dress before I give her permission to come in and check up on us.

Kenji follows right behind her and puts a stocking on his head like a cap. He looks like a pirate or a thug.

Whatever. He looks hot. I'll definitely be doing more than kissing him at midnight.

Around eleven p.m., Tiny arrives. I didn't think she would actually show up. Per our deal, she doesn't bring anyone with her. I thought for sure this would scare her off. I mean, really, who shows up to a party alone?

"Hi!" she says, giving me a big wave. She goes all out and begins to pin together an outrageous-looking outfit. Everything in the clothes pile is cut up small, and yet it still looks too big on her.

She helps herself to a beer and makes her way over to me. She is saying hello to every person, introducing herself, shaking their hands when they'll let her.

She's so painfully friendly.

"Hi!" she says, all smiles. "I knew this party would be cool."

"You made it," I say, smiling but not really feeling it.

"How'd you get here?" Kenji asks. "I didn't think you could drive."

"Sheldon drove me," she says. "I told him you lived up high in the hills, so he said he'd drive me and find a good spot to stargaze. I'm going to call him when I'm ready to go."

"Oh, brother," Kenji says.

He slides his hand into the back of my jeans and pinches me.

Perla joins us from the pile of clothes.

"I really like your dress," Tiny says, pointing underneath the elements that Perla has added to make her ensemble.

If there's one thing Perla likes, it's to be flattered.

"Thanks! So this dress is *classic*. It's vintage Patricia Field. From the *eighties*. I mean, my mom said that all the actresses want a dress like this. I'm *so* cutting edge."

"Wow," Tiny says.

Perla has this way, when she wants, of making you feel as if you're the only person in the room. She's doing it to Tiny now. She's drawing her in, as though she's telling her a secret. Tiny moves in closer; she can't help it. No one can.

"I know, right?" Perla says. "I'm probably going to be famous."

Tiny is now giving Perla that stare. She's under the spell of Perla, the one where you want to be near her, the one where you want her to be your friend so badly no matter what comes out of her mouth, because she just looks so good.

And Perla loves the attention. She lives off the adoration. And as I am watching them together, I'm surprised to see that they are actually getting along. They are really talking, about actors, movies, and directors, stuff that I know nothing about. I am almost jealous of how easily they talk to each other.

Tiny is *my* freak. Not Perla's.

I start listening again.

"Check it. I made this agreement with my dad," Perla says. "I pass my classes and then he makes me a star. He wants to create a reality show for me. I'm thinking of calling it *Perla's Party.*"

"Great title," Tiny says.

"I know, right? And then, obviously, my career will skyrocket from there—roles in major movies, guest TV appearances, my own talk show. My father says the world is my oyster."

"Wow," Tiny says. "It's so much easier for average-size people to get a break in Hollywood. Or anywhere, really."

"Oh no. She did *not* just say that!" Perla starts throwing gestures around with her attitude hands and looking at me for an explanation.

I shrug. I don't know what she's talking about. I don't know what just happened. I don't know what Tiny just said to make Perla freak out.

So Perla turns back to Tiny.

"Did you just call me *average*?"

That's the moment when everything in the room stops.

"Duh!" Tiny says. "You *are* average."

Now Tiny looks over at *me* to back *her* up.

I am standing right between them.

I look at neither of them. I look at the half-empty cup in my hand.

The word *average* is just out there, hanging in the

air like a big social mistake. Tiny doesn't know what she's done. She was just being honest.

"There is nothing *average* about me," Perla says.

"Oh no, no, no. You misunderstood me," Tiny says, laughing. "I said average *size* . . ."

But it's too late. Perla moves on because she does not understand what Tiny is saying, and now any inroad that Tiny has made is gone. Evaporated. Finished. Perla will never see Tiny as anything other than a freak. A freak who thinks *she* is average.

I could save the moment. I could clear the air. Or I could speak up and say something cutting to Perla. Perla deserves it for being so dim. But I just can't say anything without ruining my own night.

I guess I'm just selfish that way. So instead of opening my mouth, I take another big sip of beer.

I look at Tiny, who's trying very hard not to break her happy face. She doesn't understand why the attention Perla was giving her has suddenly been taken away. She doesn't understand that she can't be herself with these people. Nobody here understands her, or wants to.

But I think I do.

"Excuse me," Tiny says. "All this beer, you know. I have to use the bathroom."

"'Cause her bladder is so *small*," Perla says to me, then laughs and moves over to the snacks.

I watch as Tiny makes her way down the hallway,

but she passes the bathroom door and pulls out her cell phone. It's pretty clear she's not coming back into the party.

I know that if the shoe were on the other foot, Tiny would go out of her way to make sure I was okay. Like she did with Matthew, the Fat Boy.

"That little freak has a big set of balls," Perla says, rejoining me with a plate of food. Pink cake, sugared doughnut holes, heart-shaped cookies.

I wish I could say, "For someone so beautiful on the outside, Perla, you're ugly and average on the inside."

But it's too late to move now and do what probably would be the right thing. Tiny is gone, and the count-down begins. Now everyone at the party is too busy clinging to the person next to them as they yell the numbers backward down to one.

"HAPPY NEW YEAR!!!!!" I shout.

And then I grab Perla's hand, squeezing it a little tighter than I should.

36.

"When I was young, we all pitched in and cleaned up the day after a party."

Dad has his cranky pants on because Mom said he couldn't watch the Rose Bowl until he's finished helping me.

"You were never young," I joke.

But there is a certain new spring in his step as he scoops up plates and napkins and dumps them into the trash.

"Oh, I was, once," he says. "One New Year's Eve, I held a girl in my arms all night. Solange. I was in Paris doing my year abroad. She had the longest eyelashes."

"Dad, you are totally grossing me out," I say.

He brings over a tray of half-full beer cups, and we begin pouring out the liquid into the laundry room sink.

"When I was there, I lived in the Thirteenth, in the Parisian Chinatown. The restaurant next door to me was closed for the holidays and so they had given me bags and bags of fortune cookies. Solange and I must have opened up hundreds of fortune cookies that New Year's Eve, just to get the fortune we liked best."

"That's cheating," I say. "Only the first one counts."

"You're right," he says. "Because my life was not filled with great fame and fortune."

I suddenly remember that Dad has a tattoo of a fortune cookie on his shoulder.

He plugs in the vacuum cleaner, and if he has anything else to say about his youth, the words are sucked up by the noise in the room and the stupid grin on his face. Dad is lost in his warm memories.

He pushes the machine, forward and backward.

Forward and backward.

37.

In the car I pick up my cell phone three times to call Perla to come shopping with me. And three times I hang up the phone before I finish dialing.

I know that she will talk about herself the whole time and not let me get one word in. She will tell me how the clothes I try on would look better on her. She will bitch and moan about boys, how they love her too much or they don't love her enough. She will change the name of her reality show twelve times between the parking lot and the Forever 21.

When I hit The Grove, I immediately regret being there by myself. Everyone seems to be hanging out in groups.

And I can't decide which sweater to get.

I cave in.

I call Perla.

She meets me within the hour.

38.

"I just love having the whole day to myself," Dad says. He's reading the newspaper cover to cover these days, because with no job to go to, he has all the time in the world.

"Why don't you try to do something useful while I'm at work and clean out the garage?" Mom suggests.

"Okay," Dad says enthusiastically. "I'm on it!"

"And you," she says to me, "I expect the kitchen to be clean when I get home tonight. Ever since we let Nastja go, I'm overwhelmed. I just can't do it alone."

Her voice has this pinched tone to it all the time now. It's alarming, and I can't finish my grapefruit. The acid just sours in my stomach.

She picks up her keys, briefcase, and packed lunch and heads out the side door to the garage.

Dad and I look at each other for a minute before he sighs and says, "I love all the freedom I have, but I can't stand being stuck in the house all day. I miss having my company car."

"Do you want a ride somewhere?" I ask.

"That's nice, yeah. Can you drop me off on Vermont Ave.? Maybe I'll browse around at Skylight Books."

On the way there, I try to remember what it was like before I got my driver's license, when I was stuck in the house with only my feet to move me anywhere in the too-big city of Los Angeles.

Dad sits in the passenger seat, looking out the window. Daydreaming. Just like a little kid.

39.

Tiny runs up to us before the first bell. She's out of breath and obviously excited.

"Hi, Libby!" she says.

"Look, about New Year's," I say. "I'm sorry . . ."

"No worries."

Tiny acts as if New Year's Eve was a lifetime ago instead of only just a few days prior. She doesn't look stressed out about it at all. She just lets it roll off her.

I'm dumbfounded. But I guess it's actually *me* that's fucked up about it. She seems fine.

"I'm over it," she says. "Moving on, I signed up to help focus the lights for *Peter Pan* at the Pantages."

She grins.

I smile back.

Tiny's enthusiasm is contagious. I suddenly feel excited and I don't even know what she's talking about.

"Lighting designers need people to walk the boards sometimes. You know, stand on the stage in certain places so that they can focus the lights properly," Tiny explains. "Then you get a free ticket. So, you want to walk the boards with me?"

"Um, it's not my thing," I say, seeing Perla, Mike Dutko, Kenji, and Sid approaching. Although I'm still smiling, I want her to disappear before they get here.

"Your loss," she says, following my eyes and getting the hint. "See you later."

Tiny runs over to a group of her friends. I can tell by the way her arms fly about that she's telling them about walking the boards. In contrast to my friends, who are now leaning against their lockers like they are on heroin, acting too tired and too cool to stand on their own two feet, her friends are full of energy. They are just as excited as she is, and then they all start jumping for joy.

"Who jumps for joy?" Perla says, snapping her gum. "So. Lame."

Perla, Mike Dutko, and Kenji walk away from the scene playing out in front of us. Sid and I stand there a moment longer, watching Tiny and her friends and the fun they are having, until the bell rings.

As we start walking, Sid looks at me mischievously.

"What?" I ask.

"You know what," he says. "Let's do it."

Suddenly our pace slows at the same time as we let our friends disappear into the crowd in the hall in front of us.

And then Sid and I do it. In the hall, on the way to class.

We jump for joy.

40.

When I get home, I hear blaring rock music, coupled with strange yells and electronic beeps.

I follow the noise to the den, where my dad is

surrounded by open boxes, old composition notebooks, and binders. He's sitting on the floor, dusty and dirty, playing a primitive video game and listening to vinyl records on his old turntable. His laptop, surrounded by three to-go coffee cups, is open on the table.

He doesn't notice me come in.

"I don't think this is what Mom had in mind by cleaning out the garage."

Dad waves me over.

"See, the trick is to get that key," he says, motioning to the TV screen.

The song on the record ends. The needle lifts off the grooves and returns to its start position.

"Can you flip the record?" he says. "Careful not to scratch the vinyl. It's a rare one."

I flip the seven-inch record and place the needle on the turntable. It's Mudhoney, that old band that Sid likes. The music crackles, loud and live through the speakers.

I dance like crazy in the center of the room for a while, then I plop myself down and watch Dad and his quest for the key.

"Go do your homework or something," he says, moving the joystick up and down.

"Clean up this mess," I say.

He laughs. But he stops playing by letting his guy on the screen die.

"You're right," Dad says. "I was just taking a break."

He pulls out one of his old notebooks and begins to read.

"'November 4th, 1988. I think people who wear sweatpants all day have just given up on life. They walk their dogs, pick up laundry, go food shopping, see movies, even vote, in their soft, safe clothes, as if they can't tell the difference between sleep and life. They are only dreaming that they are comfortable.'"

"Ha. Better not tell that to Perla. She wears Juicy Couture sweats all the time."

He laughs.

Then he gets up, but instead of cleaning up, he sits in front of his laptop and starts writing. He doesn't stop. He's in the zone. I open my mouth, about to say something.

But it's his mess.

It's his life.

So I leave him alone and go up to my room. I look for something to do. I make a move to turn on my TV when I notice the zoo volunteer handbook lying on my desk.

I pick it up, lie down on my bed, and start reading.

41.

We're headed for the World of Bats, to clean the cave exhibit.

"How was focusing the boards?" I ask.

"It's *walking* the boards to focus the *lights*," Tiny says. "It was awesome. I got to stand in for all the Darling kids, so it was like I was the star of the show. I can't even tell you how great it was to stand on that stage and look out at the audience."

"But the seats were empty," I say. "So it's not the same thing."

"I have a good imagination," Tiny says, pulling out her squirt bottle of cleaner. I stop at the mouth of the cave.

"I have a good imagination too," I suddenly say. "I'm a cave dweller."

Then I start to jump around the interactive exhibit of stalactites and stalagmites.

"Sheldon, I think many unevolved alien life forms may be cave dwellers," Tiny says.

That makes Sheldon laugh. I like that he is laughing. I want to make people laugh again too. So I lift my arms up and wiggle like a cave dweller, like an unevolved alien life form.

He laughs louder, and then Tiny starts laughing too. She takes her spray bottle and crawls into the discovery tunnel.

"Commander Carpentieri goes in search of Evil Dust Bunnies," she reports from inside the tunnel. She makes her voice sound as though she's in a space suit.

Sheldon starts to pretend that he is walking on the moon. He looks goofy, his arms slowly pumping through the air.

"Aha! I've killed them!" Tiny says. She emerges and hands us the dirty paper towels.

"Good work, Commander," I say. I salute her. "You've obliterated their nest."

I pitch the paper towels into the garbage can that Sheldon is wheeling around. He looks in the can and shakes his head.

"What a shame," he whispers. "I would have liked to study those dust bunnies. You guys have no respect for the science."

"Science schmience!" Tiny says, squirting him. "We were being attacked, man!"

And then she disappears into the cave. I follow her, almost running. And even though we are acting like two-year-olds, jumping, crawling, and giggling, we are actually working. It goes by quickly, and we won't get in trouble anytime soon because we are doing our job.

And our job is actually fun.

"Here you go," Tiny says, handing me the Blue Team field book on the way down to the parking lot.

"Oh, I totally forgot. I didn't even look in the cases and take notes," I say. "I should go back. I still have half an hour before the zoo closes."

"No sweat. Sheldon did it while we were running around," Tiny says.

"You did?"

"You were on a serious mission," Sheldon says, shrugging.

Tiny elbows my hip. "You're supposed to say *Thank you, Sheldon.*"

"Oh yeah. Thank you, Sheldon."

It bothers me a little that he took the notes. Even though we're supposed to all take turns entering our observations, I've been the one doing the work in the Blue Team book since the beginning of the internship. It's been my job.

And I think I actually like it.

"You keep it," he says. "You're like the Mistress of the Field Book."

When I get home, I examine the book. Sheldon's observations are keen but unorganized. He crosses out a lot, and his writing is extremely small and unreadable.

I open the book to a blank page, and I take out my ruler. I make lines and headings and redo his work.

42.

At lunchtime, my spoon of raspberry low-fat yogurt only makes it halfway to my mouth when Perla starts speaking.

"So after I have my own reality show, I'll totally do like what other celebutantes do. Get parts in movies and, like, have my own fashion line."

"Who's going to design the clothes?" I ask.

"What do you mean?" Perla says. "I'm going to have my own reality show. I'll be famous. I'll be PERLA!"

She takes her hands and sweeps the air in front of her, like her name is already up in lights.

"I mean, you don't have any skill in design. I mean, what are *you* going to actually be *doing*? Will you be overseeing the line? Or will you be designing stuff yourself?"

"What is this? The Inquisition?" she says.

"No, Perla, I'm just wondering," I say. "I mean, what if your reality star plan doesn't pan out?"

"*Pan out* isn't in my vocabulary," Perla says. "I'm going to make it."

I think about Tiny, who actually went to a theater and walked on the stage and then raved about it all afternoon. She didn't sit around waiting for someone to hand her a career in entertainment on a silver platter. Of course, then again, it wasn't real. Those theater seats were empty. But she *did* something. She was *proactive.*

And Sheldon, going on and on about the newest images from Saturn or Mars or Jupiter or Uranus. He lugs out his telescope at night and actually looks at the stars. He subscribes to the astrobiology feeds and e-mails boring articles to Tiny and me. He gives us the night sky report every day. He observes the animals, figures them out, and tries to move like they would so he can understand them. So he can try and make sense out of LIFE.

Tiny and Sheldon are *doers.*

"You know what we are? We're slackers," I say. "We don't do shit. We have nothing going on."

"Please, girl. Speak for yourself," Perla says. "I'm like . . . a *bohemian.*"

"You don't even know what that word means," I say.

"Neither do you," Perla says. "And besides, I don't have to *know* what something means in order to *be* it."

Perla glares at me.

"Look," she says. "I don't need your negative energy all bringing me down and stuff."

And then she walks away from me.

Like I'm poison.

How did this happen? All this time I've thought I was an IT girl. Really, I am the Without-IT girl.

43.

After school, by the car, I pull out a candy bar, tear off the foil, and eat a piece of chocolate.

I shield my eyes from the sun and look across the parking lot and see Sid, slowly weaving his way through the parked cars toward me.

He takes off his hood when he gets to me. Then he pushes his messy wet hair forward.

"Do you have any hair product?" Sid asks.

"Why?"

"I just had gym and took a shower, and I forgot to bring my hair stuff."

"You should leave it," I say, reaching out and messing up his hair again. "It looks good this way."

But Sid pushes my hand away and smooths his hair forward again.

"I like my hair forward," he says.

"Why?"

"I want to be known as the kind of guy who always has the wind at his back," he says.

"You are so weird," I say.

Sid smiles.

As soon as Mike Dutko joins us, Sid slips on his earphones. Mike Dutko is kind of sulking. But I choose to ignore it. We all sit silently until Perla and Kenji arrive.

"Where were you two?" I say. "We're going to be late for the movie."

For once, Kenji doesn't pull me toward him. He doesn't even kiss my cheek. He just gets in my car and sits in the back seat next to Perla.

44.

"But it's SUNDAY," I say. "You know, FUN day? I already have plans."

"Well now it's No-Fun Sundays, because this family has to pull together," Mom says.

After sixteen years of not having any rules at all, suddenly Mom is like an army general, trying to mobilize the troops.

"This family is in crisis," she says. "We need to stay motivated."

"It's not my fault we had to budget out Nastja because Dad quit his job," I complain.

"Go clean something," she says, handing me the Swiffer.

"I am so over this," I say.

After I tie up the trash and put it in the trashcan outside, Mom appears with a big glass of iced tea.

"Here," she says. "You look hot. You've worked hard."

"I have to work this hard at the zoo," I say.

"Well, then, good, you've had practice."

"All my friends were going to The Grove today, and I had to pass because of you and your un-fun Sunday."

"You'll live," Mom says.

"You don't understand," I say. "I'm losing my cool. I'm probably going to lose all my friends."

"I do understand," Mom says. "I'm losing my cool. And feel like I'm losing my *best* friend."

She's talking about Dad. She undoes the elastic that holds back her long hair in a loose ponytail, and now it falls forward around her face and onto her shoulders. She sighs, then gathers it up again and pulls it back into a tighter bun on top of her head.

"I'm just trying to keep it together," she says.

45.

When I arrive at school the next day, I can immediately see that I missed the memo.

"Where's your pirate outfit?" Kenji asks.

Sid removes his earphones and looks up at me from under his hoodie, with the one eye not covered in a patch.

"It's Pirate Day," Perla says.

"Obviously," I say.

Perla has accessorized her pirate outfit with a green boa, so she looks not so much a pirate but like a cross between a pirate's wench and his faithful parrot.

Everyone is looking at me.

"I guess you were too *busy* to be part of the plan," Kenji says.

"Give me a second," I say.

I borrow a pair of scissors, stuff them into my bag, and go to the bathroom.

When I get there, I push open the stall door.

"Breathe, girl. They just forgot to tell you," I say.

I take off my shirt and attack it with the scissors. I rip and tie and shred.

I cut my skirt, pull it up over my boobs, and put on

the reinvented T-shirt. I adorn a headband with a Sharpie-drawn skull and crossbones and tie it around my head.

The bell rings as I rejoin the other pirates.

"Yo ho ho," I say. They look up at me, and they smile.

I can still pull it out of my ass.

46.

If an animal is in a different environment, it is an alien.

If a person is in a different environment, she is considered an alien.

I feel like an alien now. And my friends are alien to me.

I pick up my cafeteria tray.

"Where are you going?" Perla asks.

"I gotta double-check something on my report for the zoo," I say.

"It's nice to see you actually working hard at something," Sid says. "Usually you have it so easy."

"Well, there is a lot of precision in the work that we do. Sometimes I get mixed up."

This is half true. Half lie. I'm very precise when I want to be. The Blue Team field book is proof of that.

Perla and Kenji are completely uninterested. But Sid is paying attention.

"Cool," he says.

As I gather my things, Sid takes his iPod out of his bag and slips the earphones into his ears. He looks up at me as I start to go.

I just stand there. Looking at him. Thinking.

Could he be just as bored as I am?

"Well, if you have to go, *go*," Perla says.

So I go.

I push open the door to the library, a room I have barely visited in my three years of high school. The layout is unfamiliar.

I hear some laughter, and I follow the sound over to the table where Tiny is sitting. At first, no one notices me, because everyone is so enraptured with Tiny's storytelling. They are all hanging on to her every word.

In the library, Tiny is like a secret princess.

She finishes the story, and everyone erupts into laughter again. She is laughing as her eyes meet mine.

"Libby!" she says.

"Hey, I thought maybe you studied when you were in the library."

"Oh no. We hang out," she says. "Why? Are you having a problem? I'm sure someone here is an expert for whatever ails you."

Her hand sweeps over her adoring friends.

"Not really," I say.

"Do you want to join us?" she asks.

I look at all the faces I have never noticed before.

I think, it's too hard to get to know new people, to try to keep up with the smart conversation.

And I think, I don't belong here either.

I don't fit in anywhere anymore.

"No, that's okay," I say. "I'll catch you later."

47.

At my locker before last period, Tiny comes up to me.

"Do you want to come over after school?" she asks. "You've been moping around all day, and you look like you need a friend."

"I have friends," I say.

"Okay."

"I'm not moping," I say.

But I'm a liar on both counts.

"I thought maybe you could use the studying," Tiny says. "We have a biology test tomorrow, and I know I have a better time studying with someone."

"Okay," I say.

What the fuck.

After dinner we go up to Tiny's room.

"They're so . . . normal," I say.

"What?"

"Your family."

"Define *normal*, please," Tiny says.

"Tall."

"Yeah, well that's what I thought you'd say. That's what everyone says, and let me tell you something, it's bullshit. Nobody sees that I'm normal too."

I run my hand along her bookshelf. There's a jewelry box that says *Good things come in small packages.* And she's got a ton of books I've never heard of. One whole bookcase is dedicated to acting books and plays.

And on the top shelf, in front of the Shakespeare plays, is my purple shoe. The one I lost at the Fall Formal.

"Is this my shoe?" I ask.

Tiny stops organizing the study area.

"That?" she says.

"Yes, this," I say. "My shoe."

I take it off the shelf and hold it up for her to see.

"Um, it was in the hallway outside of the bathroom at Fall Formal," she explains. "You dropped it when you went in. I took it for safekeeping."

"You knew it was me?" I say.

"Everyone knew it was you," she says.

"I'm taking it back," I say.

My hand shakes as I hold the shoe, and I know that Tiny is watching me, smiling.

She's always smiling.

She thinks I'm so cool, so worth admiring.

I know that there is a part of her that would give anything to be me, even for just one day.

Why doesn't she get it? I'm not cool. And I'm not happy.

I'm not *anything*.

I don't want to have to pretend for Tiny like I do with everyone else lately. I just want to be myself. But how can a person be something as simple as herself when she doesn't even know who she is anymore?

"I have to go," I say, grabbing my books.

My pulse is racing again. Maybe I should see a doctor. Maybe my heart is weak.

"I should've told you I had the shoe," Tiny says.

"It's not about the shoe," I say.

"Then what?" Tiny asks.

"I can't explain it," I say. "I just can't."

I shove the shoe back at Tiny.

"You should throw it away. It's nothing special."

I run down the hallway and out the front door to the curb and climb into my car.

I cry into my fake-fur-covered steering wheel.

115

48.

"Where were you yesterday after school? I totally couldn't find you," Perla says.

"I went out with Tiny," I say.

"What is she, like your new best friend?"

"No," I say.

"Well, you spend a lot of time with her," Perla says.

"No, I barely even like her," I say.

But we both know that's not really true.

"What's up with you and Mike Dutko?" I ask. "He's following you around like a lovesick monkey."

"Nothing," Perla says, avoiding my eyes. "He's bugging me."

"You and Kenji seem to be hanging out a lot," I say.

"I thought you said you and Kenji were casual," Perla says carefully.

"We are," I say. "We're so casual that I hardly see him anymore."

"Kenji and I are just friends," Perla says.

Right.

49.

While Tiny and Sheldon clean Camp Gombo, the interactive safari tent exhibit, I am cleaning the outside glass of the chimpanzee cage.

Poco, one of the little guys, breaks away from the pack and climbs up onto a piece of fire hose stretched out to resemble a vine.

His dark little eyes follow my hand as I spray the window and wipe it with the rag. He is fascinated by me. I stop what I am doing and stare back at him.

We're both in cages, I think.

"You didn't get that much done," Tiny says, coming up behind me.

I break my gaze with Poco, who scampers away.

"I'm not a very good worker," I say. Then I tell the truth. "Maybe this internship was a bad idea."

I should just give this up, I think. *I am dirty and sweaty. I stink. I'm tired. I suck at this. I'm losing all my friends.*

"We'll help you," Tiny says, putting her hand on my shoulder. "We're a team, right?"

It's such a nice thing Tiny has just said. My friends

would never help. We're not a team. With them, it's everyone for themselves.

Tiny grabs one of my rags and starts spraying the bottom of the window. Sheldon follows suit, doing the higher parts.

Later, as we're walking back to the utility closet to put away the buckets and rags, Sheldon speaks up.

"Poco likes you," he says.

"What?"

"It's unusual. He's the shyest chimp of the bunch."

Great. I am liked by a chimpanzee.

That's the best I can do right now.

Nonhuman.

50.

I wake up with the need to find something to do. I call Perla and Kenji and get their voice mail. After waiting two hours for them to call me back, I give up on them.

I call Sid.

"Hi, Sid. What's up? Wanna go for a hike or something?"

"I'm about to head out for work."

"Oh."

"But I'm really glad you called," he says. "Rain check?"

"Whatever," I say.

"You should stop by the salon. I'll give you some free product."

"Um . . . maybe."

"Great. That's the other line. So, I'll see you later," he says, hanging up.

Didn't he hear me?

I said, *maybe.*

My day is turning out hopeless. There is no one to hang out with. I am forced to find fun all on my own.

In the back of my mind there is a voice reminding me that I could call Tiny, but I don't listen to it. Instead I make my way down the hall.

The sun falls squarely on Mom, sitting at the kitchen table, her head resting on her hand as she reads a magazine. Her long, long hair spills over her shoulders.

. She catches me staring at her.

"What?"

"I'm declaring a fashion emergency."

"Where?"

"On your head," I say. "You should totally get a haircut."

"Why? What's wrong with my hair?" She pats her hair protectively.

"It's old-fashioned. You look kind of like a hippie."

"Well, maybe I do need a trim." I follow her to the bathroom and lean on the doorway as she examines herself in the mirror.

I step behind her and I lift her hair up past her shoulders. "It would be so cute up, and flippy and with some highlights. We should go get you a haircut right now."

Mom opens the drawer next to the sink and takes out the scissors.

"I can trim it myself. It's not in the budget to go to the hairdresser right now."

"We can go to Rudy's. Sid works there. He'll give us a discount."

"It's Saturday," she says. "Don't you have something you would rather do?"

No. I don't have anything I would rather do. I do not want to walk around The Grove and not be able to eat lunch and not be able to buy cute new clothes and not buy a new novel and not go see a movie and then not get a latte and maybe not get some mint chocolate chip ice cream. I do not want to be bored because I don't have the money to have fun. And I definitely don't want to not do any of that all by myself.

"I'd be seeing Sid and hanging out with you," I say. "It'll be fun."

Mom puts the scissors back into their red plastic case and nods.

"Okay."

120

"Yo, yo," Sid says when we walk in. He smiles. "You came to visit me at work?"

"No, I'm here for my mom. I'm giving her a fabulous makeover."

"Sounds like you're playing dress-up," Sid says. Then he leans over the register book and whispers, "Just FYI: she's not a Barbie doll."

"I know," I say. "Just put her name on the list."

Sid sighs.

"I'll get you in as quick as possible."

"I know you will."

I wave to my mom, who is standing by the magazines, and give her a thumbs-up. Then I join her and point at pictures to show her everything I think her hair will be.

"Julietta!"

Sid finally calls my mom's name, and as she settles into the chair, I begin to give the hairdresser instructions. My mother looks uneasy. The hairdresser gets what I'm saying and begins snipping away long strands, and they fall to the ground.

"Are you sure, Libby?" Mom says.

She looks uncomfortable. Demetra, the hairdresser, stops what she's doing. She senses my mom's stress.

"Just keep cutting!" I say. "It's going to be great."

My mom is now completely freaking out as she looks in the mirror.

"You look so modern!" I say encouragingly.

But instead of agreeing with me, my mom is now crying. Demetra stops cutting. People in the other chairs begin to lean forward and look over at us. My mom is not being quiet about it.

"Mom, stop crying."

But that just makes my mom cry harder. Then she says the words that make my heart freeze.

"I look terrible."

Demetra is now horrified. She has a woman having a full-blown breakdown in her chair.

"You look fine," I say, trying to hold on to the situation. "It's just a big shock, Mom, from long to shorter."

Demetra ignores me.

"How can I fix it?" she asks my mom.

"You can't," my mom says.

"But it's awesome!" I say. "You're like a twenty-first-century beauty!"

I'm beginning to realize I don't know what I'm talking about. She might not be crying about the hair, which makes me feel kind of freaked out. I realize the last thing my mom wants is another big change in her life.

I look around at the people in their chairs with their wet hair and half-done haircuts, and they are all looking right at *me,* blaming *me* for my mother's crying. My eyes find Sid, who has finally looked up from his desk and sees that there is trouble. He leaves his post and makes his way over to us.

"Everything okay?" he asks.

He looks from my mom, who is openly crying with snot running down her nose, to Demetra, who now looks as though she is about to cry too.

He puts his hand on Demetra's shoulder. "Why don't you go get Mrs. Brin a glass of water."

Then he kneels down at my mom's feet and puts his hand on her knee, not in a pervy way, but as though he is soothing her. He whispers to her, like he's calming a skittish animal. I lean in, but I can't hear what he's saying. Eventually my mom begins to smile, and everyone in the beauty salon who seemed to be accusing me of Fashion Murder seems to sigh with relief. They turn back to admiring themselves in the mirrors.

I'm so jumpy inside that I wish Sid would do his calming trick on me. But instead he gets up off his knees and winks at me, then goes back to work and leaves me to my own devices.

"What did he say?" I ask in the car on the way home.

My mom is still smiling. Sid gave her some free product, and Demetra came back and made the cut more pixie-like. She looks pretty good.

"He said I looked chic." Mom laughed. "I think he was trying to flirt with me."

"Ew, gross," I say.

"I like Sid. He seems very nice."

"Well, if you like him so much, why don't you marry him?"

"You have gone from Fashion Freedom Fighter to Irritated Teenager in just under 2.5 hours," Mom says. Then she laughs again and shakes her new, short hair.

51.

Kenji and I are finally out alone. Even though I didn't care too much before, now that I never get to be alone with him, all I want is to be alone with him.

I watch him as I wait by the counter for my blueberry tea to be ready. His shoulders are wide and strong as he sits straight as an arrow, making his long-sleeved T-shirt fall and fold in all the right places. I'm amazed at how he makes his every body movement look so effortless. Like he's fluid. When he leans over the table to play with the sugar bowl, the bone at the nape of his neck sticks out, and I have this sudden desire to run over and kiss it.

As if he's reading my thoughts, he turns around and looks at me, smiles, and sticks out his tongue. He puts his arm up on the back of the couch.

I see myself in those arms. Tonight I'm going to get me some.

I walk toward the couch and settle myself into Kenji's embrace.

Then the door to the café opens, and Perla walks in. She beelines straight for us, pulls up a chair, and leans in close.

Kenji takes his arm off my shoulders.

"You didn't order me one?" Perla pouts.

"I forgot," Kenji says.

"Never mind—we can share." She leans over the coffee table and starts to drink from his cup.

52.

Tiny is dancing around the empty cage, using the mop as her dance partner.

"Come on, Libby!" she commands. "Dance!"

"No, thanks."

"Boring!"

Her twirling makes the color from her reconstructed T-shirt and her dirty work pants swirl.

She jetés awkwardly in the air.

I just can't see myself letting go like that today.

No. Not today.

How can anyone take Tiny seriously?

"Okay, okay, stop acting like a clown," I say.

Tiny stops dancing. Breathless, she looks at me, head cocked sideways like she knows there is something bugging me.

"You know what I wish?" she says.

"No," I say. I can't hold back the irritation in my voice. "What?"

"I wish I *was* a clown," she says.

Obviously I have a look on my face, because she points at me and laughs.

"I mean, a clown as in fool. As in player. As in actor," she says.

Tiny centers herself on a rock that sits high in the cage, and she begins to recite lines. As she struts around, she is confident, mesmerizing.

I almost forget that she is a dwarf. A freak. A tiny thing.

With those words in her mouth, she is larger than life.

When she's done, she bows.

I take off my work gloves and applaud. I can't help

myself. Tina has transformed in front of my very eyes. Even though she is back to being just Tina, she seems different.

"Who wrote that?" I ask. "It was beautiful."

"Duh, Shakespeare," she says. "Didn't you read *Romeo and Juliet* for English your freshman year?"

I don't tell her I just read the Cliff Notes and rented the movie and got a B, as usual.

Instead I say, "Bravo."

Later, Sheldon, Tina, and I are on a break getting some eats at the food stand by the Australian animals. The kangaroos are lying down, resting on the ground, while we lie resting on the benches in front of them.

"I wish I could really be center stage," Tina says.

"Well, it's kind of obvious," I say.

"An open secret," Sheldon says.

"I guess it's true. I wear my heart on my sleeve," Tina says.

"But I just don't get it," I say. "If you want to be an actress, why do you intern at the zoo? Don't you think your time would be better spent interning at a theater?"

"Because I need some skills, a career. And you know, science can be very artistic. Especially research," she says. "I just have to be realistic."

It sounds wrong, though. Like she's not really being

herself. Like those aren't her words coming out of her mouth. *I have to be realistic* sounds like something my dad used to say.

"I'm not Perla," she says. "Little People, you know, don't get a lot of parts. The Screen Actors Guild actually has us listed as disabled. My father doesn't want me to get my feelings hurt."

"But there are plenty of Little actors," I say. "Aren't there?"

"Yep," Sheldon says.

"And don't big actors get their dreams squashed and get really hurt and chewed up and spit out by Hollywood?" I say.

"Yep," Sheldon says.

"So, it sounds like everyone gets treated pretty even-steven to me."

"I keep telling Tina that she's the best actress I know," Sheldon says in his quiet way. "Did you know that she was cast in *A Midsummer Night's Dream?*"

"That play they're putting on at school?"

Tina nods. "Yeah, but they offered me the part of Puck. I wanted the part of Hermia. She's little, but she's *beautiful.*"

"Yeah, I don't know who Puck is," I say.

"The monster. The ugly monster," Tina says. "Remind me again how you are passing English?"

"Charm," I say.

"Well, they only cast me because I'm small. Let the dwarf play Puck."

"Puck's not a *monster*. Puck's a *fairy*," Sheldon says. "It's a great part. People kill to be Puck."

"I. Am. Not. Going. To. Do. It," Tina says. "The teacher in charge of the Drama Club told me to take some time to think about it. I've thought about it. I can't do it. I'm turning it down."

"Why?" I ask.

"I don't want to talk about it," she says, putting on a big, fake smile. "So, don't forget that we're car-pooling this Saturday for the volunteer zoo sleepover. Won't that be fun?"

"She's changing the subject," Sheldon says to me.

"I don't get it, Tina," I say. "You really are a great actress. The way you did that thing in the cage. Perla could never do that. I *believed* you."

"But look at me," she says.

"I *am* looking at you."

Tina sighs.

"Don't you get it, Libby? Nobody ever lets me forget I'm small. If I keep telling the universe that I can only be the monster or the elf or the fairy or the freak, then I'll never get to be the beautiful girl."

"Tina, I gotta be frank," I say. "If you keep waiting

for the perfect part, you'll never get to be an actress. But if that's what you want, then hey, go for it. Don't be in the play. Stand on the sidelines."

"You don't understand," she says.

"Yes, I do. Don't try to tell me you're not proud of who you are. You have more self-confidence than anyone I know," I say. "And you *should* be proud. You are *Tina*. You are a monster, and a fairy, and a freak. *And* a beautiful girl."

Tina throws her shoulders back and grins.

We both know I'm right.

53.

When Kenji picks me up, I notice that Perla is in the front seat, so I have to squish in the back with Sid and Mike Dutko. When we get to Jakob's house, the party is already in full swing.

I don't have anything to say to anyone. I head straight for the beer.

The music is loud, and the deck is full. Jakob's parents, Soren and Ilsa, are splashing each other in the pool.

By my third drink, I find myself in the pool in my

underwear. The warm water swirls around me. My limbs touch other limbs. I am in close contact with everyone, but I want to be alone with someone.

I swim to the side of the pool to try to pull Kenji into the water with me, but I get there just in time to see Perla pulling him seductively by the hand, leading him into the house.

And I know what that means. I can't kid myself any longer.

I get out of the pool and duck my hand into the cooler for another beer.

I scan the party to see who I could make mine. I am not going to spend the night at the party alone. But it seems as though everyone I would bother to hook up with has paired up already.

That's when I see him. Sid. He's getting into the Jacuzzi, which is occupied by a couple of girls.

I make a beeline for him.

I climb into the Jacuzzi and climb right on top of Sid. My legs wrap around his waist, and I lean toward him. He has a freckle underneath his right eye.

"What are you doing?" Sid asks.

"I'm going to kiss you, and you are going to like it."

"No," Sid says. "You're not."

I hear the girls sitting in the Jacuzzi with us start to laugh.

"What do you mean, no?"

"I don't kiss drunk girls," he says.

Then he gets out of the Jacuzzi, boner and all, and leaves me there.

54.

I arrive on Saturday afternoon to pick up Tina and Sheldon for the zoo volunteer sleepover. I am still hung over from Jakob's party. I knock on Tina's front door, and Sheldon leads me into the kitchen.

I look around. Everything is yellow, too cheerful for me today.

"Where's Tina?" I ask.

"She'll be down in a minute," he says.

Sheldon goes back to reading his magazine. Across the glossy spread is an amazing burst of stars.

"Oh!" I exclaim.

Sheldon looks up, startled. I have startled myself too.

"What is that?" I ask.

"An article on the possibility of biotas on other planets," Sheldon says.

"No, *that*," I say, pointing at the picture that is full of light and mystery.

"A nebula. It's an exploded star. Like a supernova."

"Supernova. So, yeah, what is that?" I ask again.

"A supernova is when a star explodes and becomes very luminous. It brightens in the night sky when the light from its explosion finally reaches us. A neutron star."

"It's so cool-looking," I say.

"You want to hear something cooler?" Sheldon leans to me across the table.

"Yeah, I do."

"We are constantly being bombarded with neutrinos from those stars," he says.

"So anyone could be walking around with a piece of a star in them?"

"Well, I don't know about that. But we're constantly being bombarded by stuff every day. Neutrinos slice right through the earth."

"Wow," I say.

I smile, because the thought of being bombarded with neutrinos makes me curiously happy.

"Are you *sure* you don't like science?" Sheldon asks.

"I guess it's all right," I say.

"Yeah, it is," he says, nodding. Then he buries his nose in his magazine again.

"Sorry I'm late!" Tina says, rushing into the kitchen.

As we get ready to leave, she stands next to the door and puts her hand on her head. I see the markings and realize it's a growth chart.

In true Tina fashion, she shrugs it off.

"You never know," she says. "Maybe I grew during the night."

55.

We arrive at the zoo and are taken on a nighttime tour. Base camp is at the treetops terrace, where we have a big barbecue and animal trivia contest. Sheldon beats everyone by like a million points and wins a giant stuffed gorilla. It falls short of my idea of "fun." Good thing I brought a magazine.

"What are you reading?" Sheldon asks, climbing into his sleeping bag.

"*Teen Vogue,*" I say. "I'm catching up on my cute factor."

"Yeah, I guess shoveling elephant shit isn't really the best thing for great skin."

That makes me laugh.

"That's a good one, Sheldon. You're funny."

"Yeah. I'm funny. Not just funny-looking."

It strikes me that Sheldon knows that he's not the best-looking person in the world. But it's kind of amazing how when you get to know someone, they are good-looking in their own special way. Sheldon's acne kind of disappears behind his smart brain.

I wish he liked me more.

"Why do you hate me?" I ask.

"I don't hate you. You think I hate you?"

"I always feel stupid around you."

"I don't mean to make you feel stupid," he says. "You know, I always feel uncool around you."

"The only thing uncool about you is your jeans."

"Why? What's wrong with my jeans? They're comfortable."

"Well, they make me *un*comfortable."

The red starts creeping up his neck.

"I'm sorry," I say.

"I just don't have time to waste on stuff like that. And you seem to have a lot of time to waste."

"On shopping?" I ask.

"Yeah."

"Well, I think you pride yourself on being so accepting of everyone, even aliens, and you won't even accept me as I am," I say.

"I guess I have a double standard," he says. "I'm sorry if I've made you feel bad. I'm a jerk."

"No sweat," I say. "I'm a jerk too."

We smile. It feels good to smile.

"You know," he says. "I've been meaning to tell you that you really do a good job on the field guide. I don't think we would be getting gold stars on our chart if it weren't for you. You really have an eye for observation and organization. You'd make a good scientist."

"You think?" I say. "I gotta be honest with you, Sheldon. I don't feel like I'm seeing anything right lately."

I realize that I have scooted my sleeping bag way close to Sheldon. I'm right next to him.

Tina comes out of the bathroom. She climbs into her sleeping bag, which she's moved over to the other volunteers.

Sheldon and I are alone on this side of the room. The lights go off. I wonder if I should move.

"Maybe I should go over by Tina," I say.

"No, it's okay. Stay here," Sheldon says. "We could keep talking. You could tell me what kind of jeans I should buy, or something."

Then I think, right. Now he wants to make out with me, or *something*. But now that I know that he doesn't hate me, I think maybe that would be okay. Even though he's not my type. Even though he's a pizza face.

But he just falls asleep. He doesn't touch me, or keep talking, or anything.

I wake up in the morning all mad. What's his problem? Doesn't he know? *Everybody* makes a pass at me.

Then I think, wow, maybe he was *respecting* me.

Then I think, wow, maybe he was *rejecting* me.

Then I think, wow, it's the second time I've been rejected in less than two days.

56.

"Nothing happened."

"But you slept next to him." Tina has a glint in her eye.

"Nothing happened. Gosh, he's like the only guy ever to not try to stick his tongue down my throat."

Besides Sid, I think, but I don't correct myself. And I certainly don't tell Tina that.

"Mochaccino," I say when we get up to the counter. "No whipped cream."

Tina sidles up to the barista, who is West Hollywood dreamy, and says, "I'd like a large double shot of *you*."

He laughs.

I am embarrassed. She looks back at me as we leave the store and shrugs.

"What?" she says. "If I don't make people notice

me, then they're not going to notice me. Besides, he was totally cute! You never know, maybe he would ask me out."

I don't tell her that he slipped me his phone number on a napkin and didn't charge me for my banana bread.

"You know, Sheldon is a catch," Tina says. "He's like a diamond in the rough. He's going to make someone a great boyfriend."

"I'm sure he will," I say. "But it's not going to be me."

But Tina is right. Sheldon *is* the nice guy who finishes last. He's the one you overlook. The one who's been sitting right in front of you the whole time, as plain as the nose on your face.

"Sheldon is a gentleman and a scholar. He's adventurous, loyal, kind-hearted, smart, and a good friend."

"Yeah. I just don't see it," I lie.

I know she's talking about Sheldon, but it sounds kind of like she's talking about herself.

Isn't that something they say in all those magazine quizzes? Your friends are a reflection of who you are or how you feel about yourself?

Well then, maybe I *could* like a nice guy.

57.

He is mesmerized, leaning against the fence looking straight at the orangutans when I spot him.

"Dad?"

"Look at that little guy," he says.

He is looking at an orangutan with a bag over its head.

"Maybe I should put a bag over *my* head," he says under his breath.

"Dad, are you okay?"

He pulls out a little black notebook with an elastic band around it and jots something down. Then he turns and looks at me, finally noticing that I'm there. He pulls me in for a hug.

"This was the best Christmas present you ever got me," Dad says. "The zoo passes are even better than the paperweight you made me in the first grade."

I stand with him and watch the orangutans. Just looking at them soothes me. I prop up my elbows on the fence and stare out blissfully at the apes, forgetting that I have a list of tasks to finish.

I observe the way one sits and stares at us.

Then moves to a quiet corner.

Then swings the length of the cage.

Then settles in a shady spot.

Then decides to join its friend.

Then points to the other orangutan's chest, where a piece of hard candy is stuck.

Then takes the hard candy off the other orangutan's chest and pops it into its own mouth.

"Are you on a break, Libby?" asks Mrs. Torres. She's leading a group of prospective volunteer docents through the zoo.

She's interrupted my zen.

"Oh, sorry, Mrs. Torres. This is my dad," I say.

"Hello," Dad says, sticking out his hand to shake.

"Okay," Mrs. Torres says, nodding, making her koala bear earrings tremble. Then she continues on with her tour.

But I know it's not okay.

"Guess I have to get back to my duties," I say. "See you later?"

"Yeah," Dad says. "I didn't mean to get you in trouble."

"No, no trouble. I'm glad you came."

I start to walk away, then I remember that Dad doesn't have a car.

"Dad, do you want to meet at five? I could give you a ride home."

"I'll walk home."

140

"You're *going to walk?*"

He shrugs and stands there looking like a little boy. I should bring him to the lost and found.

Then he turns back, hypnotized by the magnificent beasts and the words he's scratching into that Moleskine notebook.

true love w/ L. libby

Sheldon is hovering outside the zoo exit. He's fiddling with his shoe or something, but he looks like he's biding time. I know what he's doing. He's waiting for me.

He stands up when I get to him.

"Hey," he says.

"Hey," I say.

We both kind of stand there. He looks like he's going to explode with a stream of things to say, but instead of talking, he keeps swallowing.

What if I made it easier for him? I wait five more seconds, to give him a chance.

"Wanna go do something sometime?" I say, finally.

He smiles. Bad skin. Nice teeth. He licks his chapped lips.

"Yeah," he says. "How about I come over with my telescope later?"

"I would like that," I say, feeling a little bubble of joy float up to my mouth in the form of a smile.

"Okay," he says, and he takes my hand and squeezes it. "Thanks."

58.

It's nearly midnight.

I am standing outside at the top of my dead-end street wearing a too-thin coat. I want to take the coat off because I'm wearing a pale blue angora sweater that makes my boobs look nice, but it's too cold. No wonder Sheldon is always wearing those clothes. They might look bad, but the layers of flannel and thermal and wool must keep him warm while he's waiting for the stars and planets to rise. Maybe he's not clothes-challenged. Maybe he's just practical.

And regardless of what I think, he does actually kind of have his own style going on.

I pour myself some cocoa from the thermos Sheldon thoughtfully brought with him.

"That was so smart, to bring something hot to drink," I say.

"It gets chilly at night," Sheldon says.

He dials up numbers on the telescope.

"The great thing about your street is that there are no streetlights," Sheldon says.

He keeps looking into his telescope and not over at me. He's nervous. It kind of makes me glad that I've aroused such feelings in someone. Because the way that he tenderly cares for his telescope and the way that he gently longs for the sky is nice.

"So, can we look at the moon?" I ask, moving closer.

"Sure. But it's really bright. We should look at that last. You can get light-blinded afterward," Sheldon says.

I notice that I don't have to strain to hear Sheldon anymore. Lately it seems as though my ears have adjusted to his soft-spokenness.

Finally he finishes adjusting his telescope, and then steps away from it.

"Wanna look?"

I put my eye on the viewfinder and point myself up to the stars. I see nothing but a small, fuzzy-looking ball. It looks like a smudge on the lens.

"Am I supposed to be seeing something?"

"Mmm-hmm," Sheldon says.

"Am I looking at something that looks like a little blurry blob?" I ask.

"It's a globular cluster," Sheldon says.

"Globular cluster! Ha! That sounds like it's related to phlegm. Like someone's hocking a loogie," I say.

I stop looking in the telescope and look straight at Sheldon. I expect his look to be different. Romantic. Expectant. But it's not. It is just Sheldon.

"God, you're a hopeless stargazer," Sheldon says. "You should stick to observing animals."

"It's still romantic, don't you think?" I say. I move closer to Sheldon. He doesn't notice.

"Romantic in what way?" he asks.

"I mean, you know, it's late. The stars are out. The universe. I mean, here we are, under the stars."

And then Sheldon starts to laugh.

"Are you laughing at me?" I say.

"Well, I asked you out . . ."

"*I* asked *you* out," I say, correcting him.

"Libby. I wanted to hang out so I could talk to you. I was hoping maybe, you know, since you're like the Queen of Cool, you could show me some pointers on how to be cool enough so that Tina would like me."

"Tina!" I say. "You like *Tina*?"

"Yeah, I've liked her since I met her in fifth grade."

And then I remember the way that Sheldon looks at Tina, and I know that he never gazes at me with those soft brown eyes. He only uses that look with her.

He loves her.

I get this tightening in my chest. This squeeze of horrible envy.

I think I've hit my limit with the stargazing.

"I'm sorry if there's been a misunderstanding," he says. "Gosh. I never thought I'd be the guy stuck between two girls."

He smiles. He's like a deer caught in headlights.

That's when I start laughing. How could I ever think that I had feelings for Sheldon? He isn't my type at all.

But he could be my *friend.*

I put my arm around his shoulders like a friend, and Sheldon starts laughing too.

"Yeah, you're a real sexpot, Sheldon," I say.

"My mom always said I had it in me," he says.

"So you really like Tina?" I say.

He nods.

"Well then, Sheldon," I say. "I think you have to tell her."

59.

"Hey, Libby." Perla snaps her gum behind me. I am emptying an overfull trash bin. "I didn't realize you were a janitor."

"I'm not. It's just part of my duties to clean," I say.

"You look messy," she says. "And you smell."

I probably have dirt on my face. I push my hair out of my eyes.

"Oh, well," I say. "It *is* the zoo. I don't think the

elephants give an elephant shit about how I look or smell. They just want their hay."

"Right. So, guess what? Kenji's meeting me here. We're going to explore!"

"Cool," I say. I try not to show that it bothers me. I make my face say, *See. Me. I'm cool about it.*

"Let's hang out afterward," she says. "A three-some."

"Excellent. Oh! Sid's band is playing at The Loft. Maybe we can sneak in."

"That's not what I had in mind," she says with a wink.

I see Kenji and Perla later by the monkey cages. They are jumping around on the little stage like chimpanzees. I take off my zoo shirt, tie it around my waist, and join them.

"Hey, are you off?" Kenji says.

"Taking a break," I say.

We walk around, and I point out the animals we've worked with, but they don't really care. I tell them about all the animals, but I know they're not really listening.

"Oh, shit! Check it!" Kenji says. "That's fucking rad!"

"What?" I say. I don't see anything interesting.

Kenji runs up and pushes himself against the fence.

The sign on the cage says, THIS EXHIBIT CLOSED.

146

"It's empty," Perla says.

"Why is it empty?" Kenji asks.

"I dunno—maybe they moved the animals," I say. "Or maybe they're fixing it up. Come on. The giraffes are over this way."

But I already know what Kenji is going to do before he even does it. And part of me thinks it might be fun. Part of me would once have wanted to do it too.

"Maybe there's a new exhibit in town," Kenji says.

"Don't," I say.

"What?" Perla says.

"Don't do it, Kenji," I say.

But he's already jumped. He's on the other side of the fence, and he begins his show.

"Step right up, ladies and gentlemen, and see the Los Angeles Zoo's most dangerous animal! Man! He's violent and dangerous and highly adaptable! A warlike creature, he builds large cities and attempts to gain power over land, weather, water, and even space. Watch him sleep! Watch him eat! Watch him shit! Watch him procreate! He's a funny monkey!"

Kenji is jumping around the cage. Sleeping, eating, pretend pooping. It's hysterical. A small crowd has gathered, and they are laughing at Kenji's antics.

No zoo guards have come yet, and I feel like we're lucky. He might just get away with it.

"Okay, that's enough," I say. "Come on out. Now."

"Fuck that," Perla says. "I'm going in. That Man needs a Woman."

"Come on, Libby—don't be a pussy," Kenji says.

The thing is, I *want* to do it. It looks like *fun*.

But I work here at the zoo. I respect it. You can't just go do fun things because they're fun. Not if they are irresponsible.

Kenji and Perla are having a fake tea party. People are howling with laughter. But despite the little voice in my head telling me not to do it, that it is wrong, I also hear the voice inside me telling me that I am lame. Chicken. A pussy.

"Tiny," Perla coos. "Why don't you come in?"

I turn and notice that Tina has joined the crowd.

"Yeah, hot stuff, get over here," Kenji says.

"Me?" Tina says, taking a step forward.

"Yeah, you! You pretty little thing. Don't think the guys haven't noticed you just 'cause you're so small."

Tina takes another step forward.

"I know you've auditioned for *Midsummer*," Perla says. "But don't you want to be a star? Why be in a school play? I could put you in my reality show. We're shooting the pilot this summer. You could be one of my *friends*. I could maybe put in a good word for you, make sure you get a lot of camera time."

"Really?" Tina says. Another a step forward. Hypnotized.

"Yeah, of course. I would do that for a *friend*. I would give her a break. Let her use my connections," Perla says.

Tina hesitates.

"I didn't think you liked me," she says.

"No, I do. I *really* do," Perla says. "Libby's been talking you up and shit, telling everyone how cool you are."

Perla's lying. I never actually said anything like that. But it's working.

"Yeah, you could be our friend. Come on in and hang with us, Tiny," Kenji says, grinning.

He just wants to see if they can break her.

Tina is standing her ground.

I can't move. I can't do anything. I'm frozen. I'm transfixed by the scene unfolding in front of me. It's just like a play. And I can't figure out which way the story is going to go.

And then Perla unwraps the hot pink boa from her neck and holds it out toward Tina.

"You wanna try it on, Tiny? I bet it would look so cute on you," Perla says.

Without hesitating, Tina hops up on the fence and drops herself into the cage. She smiles up at Perla as she wraps the boa around her neck.

"See, Libby, Tiny's not a pussy. She's cool enough to come in the cage," Kenji says.

It's wrong. I know it's wrong.

But it wins.

I swing my leg over the fence.

"What's going on here?" Sheldon asks as he approaches. "Libby, what are you doing?"

"We're an exhibit. We're the Dangerous Man exhibit," Tina says. "Tell him, Libby."

"We're representing the real beasts of the world," Kenji says.

"Sheldon, these are my new friends, Kenji and Perla," Tina says.

"Tina, get out of there," Sheldon says forcefully. He's mustered up some command and he turns to me. "Don't do it, Libby."

But I ignore him and jump into the cage.

Tina looks so happy that she belongs, and I just want to throw up. She's playing human ape with Kenji and Perla, who are laughing. She thinks it's *with* her, but I know it's *at* her.

I am just standing there. I can't join in.

This isn't *fun.*

It's *terrible.*

Sheldon looks like he doesn't know what to do except turn red.

And then I see her coming toward us with a group of prospective volunteers.

Mrs. Torres.

"What's going on here?"

Kenji and Perla are scrambling out the other side of the cage, running down the road, disappearing into the crowd. They don't even look back to see if Tina and I make it out of the cage. And they certainly don't stop to help us.

I am frozen.

So is Tina.

Mrs. Torres is using her walkie-talkie to call security.

"Get out of there," Sheldon says. He's begging us to move.

Eventually I find my feet firmly planted on the ground next to Sheldon.

"What were you thinking?" He's almost yelling at us.

The walkie-talkie jumps to life as the security guard reports that Kenji and Perla have been stopped and detained.

I look at Tina. She is gray. She just did it so that stupid Perla and Kenji would think she was cool. I can see it on her face. That price is too high. It's not fair.

Suddenly, I'm not frozen anymore. I know what to do. I pull the boa from Tina's neck and wrap it around mine.

"Why did you do it?" Mrs. Torres asks. "You know I have to report both of you."

"Tina didn't do it. She was trying to get me out of there," I say.

151

"That's not true," Tina says.

"Yes it is, Mrs. Torres," I say. "I'm the one to blame. The whole thing was my idea. They don't even like her. They're *my* friends."

Mrs. Torres looks at me as though I just killed someone.

"Then I'm very, very sorry for you," she says. "Tina, Sheldon, please go back to your duties."

I watch them head up the path, leaving me alone with Mrs. Torres.

"That was a stupid move, Libby," Mrs. Torres says.

"I'm really sorry," I say.

"You keep very bad company," she says. "With friends like those . . ."

"I know," I say. "I said I'm sorry."

"Sorry doesn't cut it," Mrs. Torres says. "You're out of the program. Get your things and get out."

When I get to the parking lot, Tina and Sheldon are waiting for me by my car.

"Why did you lie?" Tina asks.

A million things cross my mind.

"I don't know why I do anything these days," I say.

Tina sighs. She looks up at me. She puts her hand on my arm.

"You're such a good friend," she says. She comes up

on her tippy toes and hugs me. "Don't ever do something stupid like that again."

"You don't need anybody to help you be a star, Tina," I say. "You're already a star to a lot of people."

Sheldon stares at me, like he's seeing something for the first time.

60.

Ms. Lew calls me into her office.

"You realize that you are automatically failing your internship."

"Yes."

"And you won't get a passing grade in this biology class."

"Yes."

"You'll have to make it up in summer school."

"I understand," I say.

"I am terribly disappointed in you, Libby."

"I know."

I wait until I hear the door click behind me and I am alone in the hallway before I start to cry.

When I get home, I find Dad sitting on the couch in the rec room playing his video game. He doesn't say anything to me. He just hands me the other joystick and we look for keys.

"I'm blocked," he says. "Everything I write is shit. I don't know why I'm bothering. I should just accept the fact that I'm not an artist anymore. I'm a businessman."

Hours go by before Mom comes home late from work and finds us in the dark rec room. Neither one of us bothered to turn on the light as the sun set.

"So I just got a message about what happened at the zoo," Mom says.

The television monitor flashes GAME OVER. I hit *restart*.

"You are grounded indefinitely," Mom says.

"It wasn't really me. It was Perla and Kenji that were in the cage. I just followed. *I* didn't want to do it. I *knew* it was wrong."

"But you did it anyway, even when you knew it was wrong."

"I didn't want to be a wimp. And I wanted to save Tina."

"Excuses, excuses," she says. "You're grounded."

"Great. Why don't you try grounding me and meaning it this time?"

"What's *that* supposed to mean?" Mom asks.

"It means, I don't believe you when you say I'm grounded. You never make it stick."

She storms out of the room.

"Wanna tell me what happened?" Dad finally asks.

So I tell him. Everything.

"And the worst part," I say, "is that I actually like the zoo. After all that time of thinking it was kind of lame, and I was kind of better than it, I really like it."

Dad rubs his hand over his face.

"How about this Libby?" Dad says. "I'll try if you try."

"Okay," I say, but I don't really know what he means.

He gets up off the couch, goes to his desk, pulls out a thick manila folder, and puts his laptop into its bag.

"Neil's theater company is having its monthly new works meeting tonight," he says. "Maybe I'll drop in. Show them what I've got so far. Not worry so much about what's not working."

Now I know what he means.

61.

"I don't understand why you are being so lame about the zoo thing," Kenji says, cornering me by my locker. "Who cares?"

"I care!" I say. "Unlike you. You don't care about anything. And you don't know anything about anything. You could've brought your dirty human diseases in there. You could have germs on your shoes, on your hands. . . . Animals are sensitive. They can catch stuff. God, it was so irresponsible of you!"

"This coming from the girl who takes off her clothes at school dances and gets drunk at the drop of a hat. The Cut Queen of Hollywood."

"It's different," I say. "You used Tina."

"Oh, please," Kenji says. "In the old days, you'd have been *in* on the joke. Now, you *are* the joke."

"I'd rather be a joke than a loser," I say.

"What's up?"

It's Sid, who's come up behind me while I'm sitting by myself at lunch, for like the first time ever.

"Oh, are you talking to me? I thought I was being ignored by everyone."

"I'm my own person, man, dig it?"

"Yeah."

He looks down at his feet. Then back up at me.

"It's going to be okay," he says. "You're going to get through this."

"How do you know?" I say.

"Because I know you," Sid says.

How can he know me? I don't even know me anymore.

He pulls the earphones he has slung around his neck and offers them to me.

"Listen to this," he says.

"Okay," I say. I put the earphones in.

He presses a button, and my ears come alive. The music is melodic and hopeful and tender and delicate.

"Did you write that?" I ask.

He nods.

"What's it called?" I ask.

"It doesn't have a name," he says. "What do you think it's called?"

I think for a moment. The bell rings. The hallway floods with people moving from one room to another.

"'Rare Birds,'" I say.

"That's a good one," Sid says. "Very original."

He takes the headphones back from me and walks off to class. Even in the crowded hallway, I notice, he stands out.

62.

I follow the laughter in the library like bread crumbs, which lead me straight to Tina.

I stand quietly by the shelves until she notices me and hushes everyone up.

"Everybody, this is my very good friend, Libby," Tina says. Then she motions for someone to get me a chair, and where there was no room at the table before, now there is a special place just for me.

I sit.

I open my yogurt. But I can't eat.

"Do you remember when we were working with the tapir?" I ask.

"Yeah," Tina says.

"That was like one of the most fun days I ever had in my life."

"It's too bad that they're an endangered species," she says.

"You know what I think?" I ask.

"What?"

"I think we're all kind of like that. We're all kind of endangered."

"Are you okay?" Tina asks.

"I thought that the zoo was the stupidest thing that ever happened to me. I hated it. I didn't even like you, really. I was pretending. I was just fulfilling my duty, 'cause I signed up for it. 'Cause everything else seemed so boring. But now, everything seems boring if I *don't* get to go to the zoo. The zoo. Being responsible. Using my brain. That's been the best, most important thing I've ever done."

"It is pretty cool," Tina says.

"What am I going to do now?"

"Maybe you should take your own advice."

"What do you mean?" I ask.

"Like you told Sheldon to tell me he liked me," she says. "You should tell Mrs. Torres how much you love working at the zoo."

When she says this, my heart floods with warmth.

Tina is right. I should take my own advice.

I have to *do* something. I have to tell Mrs. Torres how I feel. I have to *try*.

63.

"What are you doing here?" Mrs. Torres asks. "I thought we had this conversation the other day. You put the animals in jeopardy with your friends. You're excused from this internship. End of story."

"I know," I said. "I just thought maybe I could still come and help. You know, without the grade."

"No."

"Then can I come back?"

"What?" she says.

"Can I do the next internship?"

"Why are you doing this, Libby?" Mrs. Torres asks.

"Because I love working at the zoo. I couldn't admit it before. I was stupid. And now I won't be stupid like that again. And when a person knows, I mean, *really knows,* that they have been galactically stupid and they want to try again, you should give them another chance."

"Libby, you do good work."

"Really?"

"But you can't finish this internship. You fail this round. However, I might consider letting you do it over," Mrs. Torres says.

"Really?"

"Let's call it a probation."

I go outside and find Sheldon and Tina.

"Hey," Sheldon comes up to me. "What are you doing here?"

"Did it work?" Tina asks. "Are you back on Blue Team?"

"Not officially," I say. "But I can come back to the zoo."

"Cool," Tina says. "We're on gnu duty today. Want to watch us work?"

"Yeah, I'll give you pointers from the bench."

64.

Mom is smiling sitting right next to Dad in the breakfast nook. She pushes the newspaper over to me.

"Look," she says.

There is an article about the Alphaville Theater collective, and in the middle of the article it says that they are doing a staged reading of a "hot new play" by Mitchell Brin.

"Wow," I say. "I'm so proud of you, Dad."

"I feel good," Dad says, smiling. He puts his arm

around Mom. "It was good to have the support of you girls while I did this."

"Yes," Mom says. "And I'm glad you're taking on some freelance work. That makes me feel less crazy."

My eyes linger on the newspaper. I flip the pages till I reach my horoscope. I want to know how my day is going to be.

But I don't read it, because the column next to it, "This Week in Science," catches my eye instead.

That's what gives me the idea for tonight's fun.

65.

It's eight-thirty p.m., and for the first time I've done all my homework. I didn't know that I could feel so good about something so simple. But there it is, all easily done without that much more effort than usual, and I feel settled inside. Accomplished.

I pick up the phone and call Sheldon.

"Hey, Sheldon. Did you read about Gruener-Wild in the newspaper today?"

"Yeah."

"It's going to be visible at ten p.m. I thought maybe

we could gather the troops and go over to the observatory and set up your telescope."

"I thought you were grounded," Sheldon says.

"Not really," I say. "Some things never change."

"I'll get Tina and meet you there. Wear a sweater."

I go to my closet and I get a ski cap and a sweater. Then I go back and I get an extra one. When in the field, scientists must dress appropriately.

On my way to the observatory, I make a stop. I park the car in front of a modest house. I count three windows over and then pick up a pebble from the ground.

I throw the pebble at the window. It taps against the glass.

I'm afraid, but I get up and go over to the window and stand under it. Finally, Sid appears.

"Hey," I say. "Come down."

"What do you want?" he whispers.

I wave for him to come down. He throws his hands up in the air, frustrated. I wave again.

He disappears from the window, and after a few minutes, the door opens and he emerges.

"What?" he says. "It's a school night."

"I want to show you something."

"Okay, show me."

"Not here. At the park."

"You want me to come with you?"

"Yeah. There's a star party at the observatory."

The night chill gets to Sid. He rubs warmth into his arms.

"I should go get dressed," he says.

"No, I brought you a sweater, and I have a blanket."

"What is it? Like a moon picnic?"

I smile.

He so gets it.

When we get to the observatory, there are crowds already gathering around telescopes set up on the lawn. Sid and I weave in and out of the throngs until we find Sheldon and Tina.

Sheldon has already set up his telescope. He and Tina are lying together on the blanket they have spread out on the lawn.

"Hi, Sid," Tina says. "This is my boyfriend, Sheldon."

"Hi, Sheldon, nice to meet you," Sid says.

Sid looks around at the crowds.

"Wow. Some party," he says.

Sheldon looks at his watch.

"Should be a couple of minutes," he says.

I dig into my bag and pull out a bottle of sparkling apple cider and pass out cups.

"So I spoke to the Drama Club advisor, and she's

going to let me share the part of Puck with the other girl," Tina says.

"That's great," I say. "Let me know if you need to run lines or anything."

"That's really thoughtful," Tina says.

"That's what friends are for," I say.

The crowd starts oohing and aahing. Strangers point into the sky.

"Showtime," Sheldon says.

My eyes follow the pointing fingers.

"I don't see anything," Sid says, looking at the sky.

"Here, look through the telescope," Sheldon says.

"What is it?" Sid asks. "A smudge?"

"It's a comet," I say.

"I thought comets had tails, like a big streak in the sky," Sid says.

"A comet has a nucleus of rock and ice, and as it nears the sun on its orbit, the ice begins to evaporate, making a tail," Sheldon explains. "Its distance from the sun and to us affects the tail and how we see it."

"Astronomers think that this comet was here before, like four hundred years ago," I add.

"Back then, comets were feared," Tina says. "When one appeared in the sky, people thought it meant that there'd be a famine, or a plague, or that it heralded the death of a king or a queen."

Sid looks up from the telescope, right at me.

"Wow," he says. "Amazing."

"I think this comet is a *good* omen," I say. "A sign of change."

"Me too," Tina says, putting her arm around me.

I can't help smiling.

The Queen of Cool is dead, I think.

Long live the Queen.

A Conversation with Cecil Castellucci

When you wrote your first novel, *Boy Proof,* did you envision the successive novels, *The Queen of Cool* and *Beige* (May 2007), forming a related trilogy?

It was actually when I wrote *The Queen of Cool* that I had another idea for a novel that would take place in the Silverlake area of Los Angeles and would have to do with music. That's when I started referring to all of the books as my Los Angeles Trilogy. I think of these books as loosely collected novels about girls in Los Angeles, with the city as the thread. They also highlight three areas of L.A.: the movie industry *(Boy Proof)*, the sciences *(The Queen of Cool)*, and the music scene *(Beige)*.

Why do you think readers identify with Libby?

All of my main characters—Egg from *Boy Proof,* Libby from *The Queen of Cool,* and Katy from *Beige*—are girls who have been one way for a long time and find out that they are actually totally different from what they thought. They all let their guard down and allow themselves to become who they really are.

Libby specifically has the cloak of cool pulled around her. She's the fearless leader of her group but is afraid to admit what's really wrong—that she's totally bored. I think that every girl has felt like Libby, totally cool in one situation and uncool in another. She's the ultimate insider and the biggest mean girl, but she also has a secret—she's a freak! The truth is, a person is only boring or uncool if they aren't being one hundred percent true to themselves.

Finding your own identity seems to be a major theme in each of your novels. Why is that?

I think identity is something that everyone struggles with at one point or another, whether they are young or old. I am always interested in that moment when a person decides who they are and what kind of person they are going to be. One of the first major times that happens, I think, is in adolescence.

What's your writing regimen?

I am a plunger, not a plotter. The story bursts out of my head like Athena did from Zeus's. I pretty much know how a story starts and where it ends. Then I follow the characters. I am also a binge writer. I'll spend days being cranky and taking hikes in Griffith Park and moping and eating chocolate and staring at the ceiling and taking baths and doing the dishes. All that time, I am gestating, pulling the threads of the story together, keeping my mind's eye on the characters, getting to know the nuances of the story—basically working it out. Then I will suddenly be compelled to write in a flurry and fit of hours and hours and sometimes a day or two. Then lather, rinse, repeat.

What is your favorite sentence from *The Queen of Cool*?

"Then I put my head down on the desk. It smells like pencil and hand." I love this line.

What attracts you most to writing for teens?

Adolescence is a time when you throw down about what kind of a person you are going to become. Emotions and feelings and everything run really high, right under the skin, and everything is pretty much the first time. I find that endlessly fascinating.

★ "A geek-chic fairy tale."

—*Bulletin of the Center for Children's Books* (starred review)

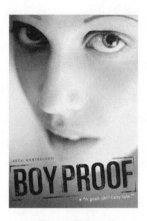

Boy Proof

Cecil Castellucci

Egg can't be bothered with friends—much less members of the opposite sex. As far as she's concerned, she's boy proof. And she likes it that way.

A BOOK SENSE 76 SELECTION

AN AMERICAN LIBRARY ASSOCIATION
BEST BOOK FOR YOUNG ADULTS

★ "Egg's journey is one readers won't want to miss."

—*Publishers Weekly* (starred review)

Hardcover ISBN 978-0-7636-2333-3
Paperback ISBN 978-0-7636-2796-6

READ CECIL CASTELLUCCI'S LATEST NOVEL

Beige

When Katy is forced to stay with her father for two weeks, she figures she'll grin and bear it. What else can a nice, polite girl do when her father, who has been absent for years, is not only a recovered addict but also the drummer of the infamous punk band Suck?

Hardcover ISBN 978-0-7636-3066-9